Heather rested her elbows on the ship's railing and stared outward, her mind filling with a sense of purpose and commitment. "Thanks for talking to me, Ian. I feel much better now. All because of you."

He too leaned against the rail, his large, rough hands inches away from her soft, smooth skin. "It was my pleasure, Heather. We're all on the journey of a lifetime. God is our shepherd, and we have only to do what he asks of us. Kindness for one another, love for each other, that is what will change the world. Medicine can heal the body. But only God can make well the human soul."

His words touched her, and her heart swelled. "I think we're going to be good friends, Ian McCollum."

"You can count on it, lass. Yes, you can count on it."

Angel of Mercy

Lurlene McDaniel

Angel of Mercy

BANTAM BOOKS
NEW YORK • TORONTO • LONDON • SYDNEY • AUCKLAND

RL: 5.7, AGES 012 AND UP

ANGEL OF MERCY

A Bantam Book / July 2001

ISBN: 0-553-57083-8

Visit us on the Web! www.randomhouse.com/teens
Educators and librarians, for a variety of teaching tools, visit us at
www.randomhouse.com/teachers

Check out Lurlene McDaniel's Web site!
www.lurlenemcdaniel.com

Published simultaneously in the United States and Canada

Bantam Books is an imprint of Random House Children's Books, a
division of Random House, Inc. BANTAM BOOKS and the rooster
colophon are registered trademarks of Random House, Inc. Bantam
Books, 1540 Broadway, New York, New York 10036.

PRINTED IN THE UNITED STATES OF AMERICA

OPM   10 9 8 7 6 5 4 3 2 1

Then the Lord said to Cain, "Where is your brother Abel?"

"I don't know," he replied. "Am I my brother's keeper?"

Genesis 4:9
(NIV)

Therefore go and make disciples of all nations, baptizing them in the name of the Father and of the Son and of the Holy Spirit. . . .

Matthew 28:19
(NIV)

To My Readers,

This book is close to my heart. Two years ago, I accompanied a missionary team to Uganda. There, I met extraordinary people—missionaries, doctors, and American kids who were working in extreme conditions to help make a difference in the lives of others.

I would like to thank them all for inspiring me with their selfless courage. And I especially thank Dr. Henry Krabbendam of Covenant College and the Africa Christian Training Institute; my son, Erik McDaniel, a youth pastor in Anniston, Alabama, who regularly takes kids on mission trips to developing countries; Benjamin Jacobs, a student at Ole Miss, who served on the Mercy Ship Anastasis; and Dr. Monte Wilson, director of Global Impact Ministries, for their input in helping me create this work of fiction. I hope this book will enable readers to experience different cultures and different ways of looking at the human condition.

If you are interested in learning more about the Mercy Ship ministry, contact:

Youth with a Mission
MERCY SHIPS
P.O. Box 2020
Lindale, TX 75771-2020

1

"I can't believe you're giving up your entire summer *and* fall instead of going to college, Heather. I mean, it's like forever! And just look where you'll be living. How can you stand it? There's no room to move, no privacy either!"

"I'll be home in time for Christmas," Heather Barlow reminded her sixteen-year-old sister, Amber. "And I don't care about the living conditions. As for college, I'll start in January. You'll hardly know I'm gone."

At eighteen, Heather was going off on a Mercy Ship to work in Africa, to try to make a difference in a place where children starved to death or died from terrible illnesses. She had grown up wanting to do something worthwhile with her life, but now that she was actually on board the ship, now that it was almost time to say goodbye to her family, Heather was beginning to feel the clutch of self-doubt. And Amber's reluctance to see her leave wasn't helping.

Amber glanced around the cramped quarters. "It's just so—so primitive."

Ignoring Amber's complaints, Heather opened her duffel bags and began putting her clothes into the narrow drawers of the dresser bolted to the wall. She would be sharing this old-fashioned small stateroom with a Swedish girl named Ingrid, whom she'd not yet met.

Across the narrow room, Amber seated herself on a bed attached by cables to the metal wall of the ship. "Ugh! This mattress is so thin, I can feel the springs."

"It's a hospital ship, sis, not a luxury liner anymore," Heather reminded her.

Years before, *Anastasis* had served as a cruise ship. But in the mid-1980s, it had been converted into a floating hospital, with three operating rooms, a dental clinic, a laboratory, and an X-ray unit. The aging ship, painted white from bow to stern, was more than five hundred feet long and nine stories high. Its staterooms, once luxurious quarters for wealthy travelers, now housed crew and staff—175 volunteers who paid their own expenses and agreed to serve a tour of duty as the ship sailed from port to port, bringing life-saving medical services to countries ravaged by disease, famine, war, and poverty.

Long-term crew members—missionary and medical personnel and their families who had signed up for extended tours of duty—were housed in the more spacious upper-deck staterooms, while short-term volunteers such as Heather were assigned the smaller rooms. The ship's once-elegant lounge and dining areas served as conference rooms and training centers. Children of the crew and staff attended school on board.

Once the ship dropped anchor in a port, engineers, carpenters, teachers, and evangelists took medical and dental services and supplies into remote areas and inland villages. They built schools, hospitals, and housing, all with donated goods. The Mercy Ship was a floating hospital. And a vision of hope.

"Well, I think it's a dumb idea to even be going on this trip, and I don't know why you want to go in the first place," Amber said, voicing her displeasure once again. "I'll bet there's no decent guys to date, and nowhere to go even if there were."

Heather sighed. It irritated her when Amber sounded so frivolous. Why couldn't she understand how important this trip was? Heather had spent so much time thinking about the trip, a whole year planning it, and ten days in May at a special boot camp preparing for it. She asked, "Are you trying to make me feel guilty? Because I won't. I've wanted to do this for a long time, and you know it."

Amber scuffed her fashionable shoes on the floor. "I'm going to miss you," she said quietly.

"I'll miss you, too." Heather saw tears shimmering in her sister's green eyes. "Hey, what's this? I thought you'd be glad to have the house to yourself. And no big sister to be in your way when school starts, either. You always said you couldn't wait until me and my friends were out of high school so that you and your friends could have the halls all to yourself." Heather sat beside Amber on the bunk and put her arm around Amber's shoulders.

"What fun is there in being home by myself? Mom and Dad won't have anything to do but go to work. And grouse at me, of course. You're the one they think is perfect in this family, you know."

"They grouse at you now," Heather teased gently. "So what will be different?"

"You won't be there to get them off my case."

"Then don't do anything to get them on your case." Heather gave Amber a squeeze. "Honestly, I really do think you go out of your way to provoke them sometimes."

"If you mean I like to have fun instead of trying to save the world, then guilty as charged." Amber sniffed and slumped lower on the bunk.

Heather did feel sorry for her sister. Their parents were both highly successful plastic surgeons—their father a wizard in facial reconstruction, their mother a respected specialist in body reshaping. True, much of their practice these days was given over to cosmetic facelifts, liposuction, and cellulite reduction, but they still were renowned for their ability to help the horribly deformed or tragically maimed. Their busy schedules left them with little free time at home. With Heather gone, Amber would be pretty much on her own. *She has tons of friends and her senior year coming up*, Heather reminded herself. Amber would be fine.

Heather scooted off the bunk. "Look, sis, Mom and Dad will be back from their tour any second now, so please help me out. No pity party, okay? I'll start to cry, and that wouldn't be good. I promise I'll write often. And don't forget, you all are going to spend a week touring Europe before you have to fly home. That should be fun."

The ship was docked in London, taking on supplies, and would sail in two weeks for the coast of Kenya. From there, Heather would accompany a special team to Lwereo in central Uganda, where she would work as an aide in the only hospital for the entire district—a hospital staffed by Irish missionary doctors. Heather's team would also build a dormitory for an orphanage run by Americans. In December, she was to fly directly home, arriving the week before Christmas.

"A week in Europe . . . whoopee," Amber said glumly. "My idea of fun isn't tracking through museums and art galleries. Mom's already got a list this long." She held her hand above her head. "Is there even one dance club on the list? I think not."

Heather laughed. "Can you see Dad moshing on a dance floor?"

A smile lit Amber's teary eyes.

Encouraged, Heather asked, "Or how about Mom fighting her way to the bathrooms? Both of them could get hurt twisting their way through such crowds. Who'd do surgery on the surgeons?"

Just then the cabin door opened and their parents stepped in. Amber quickly wiped her eyes, and Heather got up to meet them, not wanting them to see Amber's distress.

"Great tour," their father said. "You're in good hands. Excellent ORs—state-of-the-art— on a par with the ones I use in Miami."

"I'm glad you approve."

Her mother looked apprehensive. "Now I know how my mother felt when she was seeing me off to Guatemala when I was twenty-two." Heather and Amber's parents had met years before in the Peace Corps, and their stories of their adventures had inspired Heather all her life. The seeds of her desire to help the underprivileged had been planted early.

"It won't be easy, you know," her mother added. "You'll see things that will break your heart. It doesn't take much to have your idealism crushed."

"It's too late to turn back now. I'll be fine, Mom," Heather insisted, feeling more unsure than she sounded.

"Of course you will," her father agreed, sending her a confident smile. Still, she could tell by the look in her parents' eyes that they were nervous about sending her halfway around the world. "We're proud of you, honey."

A deep blast of a horn, followed by the command "All ashore" over the PA system, made them all jump. Heather's heart thudded.

"I guess that's us," her mom said. She hugged her daughter, then held her hand while they climbed the network of ladderlike stairs from the lower staterooms to the upper decks.

Topside, the June breeze felt cool. The open deck was crowded by other travelers, all in stages of telling families and loved ones goodbye. "This is it," Heather said, almost losing her nerve and following them down the gangplank to the dock below.

"You write," her mother said.

"And e-mail on that laptop I gave you," her father said, giving her a smothering bear hug.

She kissed the three of them one last time, then watched as they left. On the dock, they stood with a throng of people, waving and calling goodbye. Tears filled Heather's eyes. All at once, the six months away from home and from all she'd ever known loomed like an eternity.

The ship towered above the dock, making them look small and insignificant amid the hustling dockworkers and their equipment. Heather watched her parents and sister climb into a cab. Hanging out the window, Amber blew her a kiss. A lump the size of a fist clogged Heather's throat, while a breeze from the sea pushed her thick hair away from her face. Tears trickled unchecked down her cheeks.

Lost in sadness, she didn't realize that anyone was standing next to her until a deep male voice with a soft Scottish accent said, "It seems that your eyes have sprung a leak there, lass. Could I offer you my handkerchief to help mop it up?"

2

Heather swiped at her moist cheeks. She turned to face a young man with red hair and eyes the deep blue color of the ocean. He wore a sympathetic smile and held out a clean white handkerchief. Dazzled by his smile, she said, "I—I'll be all right."

"Here." He tucked the white cloth into her hand. "I've never met a lass who had a tissue when the waterworks started." His tone was gentle, his accent musical.

She dutifully dabbed at her tears to please him.

"Come, walk with me," he said, offering his arm. "It's better on the far side of the ship where you can look out over the water. Makes you forget your ties to the land."

She tucked her arm into his, and his large, warm hand clasped around hers. Together they strolled toward the ship's stern, away from the sight of her family's cab driving off.

"Your first trip over?" he asked.

"Yes." Heather was certain he thought her a big baby. Here she was bawling like a kid whose mommy had left her on the first day of school. "How about you?"

"My third." He nodded at her. "Ian McCollum, Edinburgh, Scotland."

She introduced herself.

"Heather . . ." He rolled her name around on his tongue as if tasting it. "Like the heather on the moors. And just as pretty, too."

She blushed, and he grinned. "In a few days you'll be so busy you won't have time to miss anybody."

"I know you're right. I didn't mean to get all sentimental. I've been wanting to do this for years, so please don't think I have any regrets about leaving."

"It's a good cause," he said. "I keep coming back to work between semesters at university."

"Where do you go to college?"

"I'm a medical student at Oxford," he said, then added, "Seminary student, too."

His soft accent fascinated Heather. She caught herself staring at his mouth as he spoke.

"Is something the matter with my words, lass?"

She felt her cheeks flush. "Uh—no . . . of course not. A doctor *and* a minister?" she asked quickly. "My parents are both doctors in Florida, and believe me, their practice keeps them busy all the time. How can you do both?"

"In truth, I cannot separate the two callings. To heal the body and not touch the soul—well, I could not do it. Physical healing is a fine thing, but to open the gates of heaven for a person . . . ah, well, that's the greater thing."

"I guess it's a little different for me," she said. "Mom and Dad were both in the Peace Corps—it's where they met, and they've always taught my sister and me that those who have been blessed by God should be generous. And I don't just mean by giving money away either. I think it's important to give of yourself, to do something worthwhile for others. I think of people as God's hands on Earth. A person shouldn't waste her life, or her blessings. You know what I mean?"

"Yes. It's more blessed to give than to receive."

"Ever since I can remember, I've wanted to make a difference in the world. I've wanted to go out and *do* something meaningful with my life. When I was a kid, at Halloween—" She broke off. "I'm sorry, I'm babbling."

"No. It's interesting. What did you do on Halloween?"

By now they had reached the far side of the ship, and they stood at the rail, looking out at the sea. "When other kids were out collecting candy, I collected money for UNICEF. It always made me feel really good to mail in that donation. I'd think about all the starving children I was helping. Kids in my classes thought I was crazy, but I didn't care. It was what I wanted to do."

"You have a sweet and gentle spirit, Heather."

She shrugged self-consciously. Sometimes she wished she were different. More like others her age. In grade school, she had been known as the school's do-gooder and was often teased about it. In high school, kids seemed more understanding, especially when she'd organized a food drive for a Miami homeless shelter and organized a clothing drive for hurricane victims and had been written up in the newspaper for her efforts. Two summers before, she'd been a candy striper at her community hospital and had loved it.

"I get sappy over a Hallmark card commercial," she confessed, then wondered if he even understood what she was talking about. "You know . . . I cry over anything that gets inside my heart. Sad movies, sad books."

"Don't think badly of yourself because you have a tender heart. Such hearts are needed in this world today. You will be touched many times when you go into the bush, Heather, lass. There are many in great need."

"I guess you'd know since you've done this before."

"Like you, I can't help myself. It's my destiny. To make people's bodies whole. To tell them about God and his love for them."

Ian McCollum's purpose sounded loftier than hers because it was double-edged. Once, when she and Amber were younger, in a fit of jealousy, Amber had hurled an accusation at Heather: "You just do this to get attention, you know. It's your way of getting Mom and Dad to take the time to notice you."

"And what's your way? To be as bad as you can be?" Heather had fired back.

Over time, she had often thought that there was a grain of truth in both her words and Amber's. She turned toward Ian. "What area of medicine are you interested in practicing?"

"Hands-on," he said with a grin. "I could

never be stuck in a stuffy laboratory, or even an operating room, day after day. Out in the bush, children die every day from things that are totally preventable. Stomach parasites, measles, whooping cough—illnesses that a simple vaccination or the right antibiotic can prevent."

"That bothers me, too. Knowing that kids die from things that are preventable. Mom told me how it frustrated her when she was in Central America to see little kids die from dehydration. They couldn't drink the water because it was contaminated. When they did, they died."

"It's a sad thing to see. When I've come before, I've stayed here on the Great White Ship—that's what the locals call the *Anastasis*—but this time, I'll be taking vaccines and supplies into Uganda."

"You're going to Uganda? So am I." The news pleased her. She liked this man from Scotland.

"Then we'll be seeing more of each other," Ian told her with a broad smile. "Once people in the bush know we're there, they'll come for miles, walk for days to see us."

"My mother told me not to expect to find much access to a phone. How does the news get around?"

"We're spoiled in the West. We think phones and computers and television are the only ways to communicate." He laughed dryly. "But news can travel in many ways, and in Africa, it travels quickly. Legend has it that the wind carries it along. And that only the ears of those born in Africa can hear it."

"I wish we could start tomorrow," she said impatiently. It would take a month to sail around the Cape of Good Hope and into the port at Kenya. "I can't wait to get there."

"It'll be here soon enough. In Africa time, as we keep it, doesn't exist. It drives Westerners crazy. No one sticks to a schedule."

She thought of her life in America, which ran by the clock. There were bells for class changes at school and schedules for planes, buses, movies, TV programs—the list was endless. She got tired of it. "Schedules are overrated," she said with a wave of her hand. "Maybe the people of Africa are on to something. The sun and the moon are the only clocks we need. Moontime—I like the sound of that, don't you?"

"You're smiling," Ian said, lifting her chin. "Makes your face even prettier."

She blushed. "You know, an hour ago my six months away from home seemed like forever.

Now, after talking to you, it hardly seems like enough time to get everything done."

"Ah, lass," he said with a bemused shake of his head. "A lifetime isn't long enough to get everything done. The time you spend here will change your life. It changed mine. You will not go back the same girl as when you left."

Already Heather felt different. Having him talk to her as if her ideas and plans mattered, as if her feelings were normal, not weird, made her feel wonderful. Back home, none of her friends understood her. Why, not even her own sister had caught on. How odd that here, a world away from all she had ever known, she had found someone who felt and thought the way she did.

She rested her elbows on the ship's railing and stared outward, her mind filling with a sense of purpose and commitment. "Thanks for talking to me, Ian. I feel much better now. All because of you."

He too leaned against the rail, his large, rough hands inches away from her soft, smooth skin. "It was my pleasure, Heather. We're all on the journey of a lifetime. God is our shepherd, and we have only to do what he asks of us. Kindness for one another, love for each other, that is what will change the world. Medicine can heal the body. But only God can make well the human soul."

His words touched her, and her heart swelled. "I think we're going to be good friends, Ian McCollum."

"You can count on it, lass. Yes, you can count on it."

3

Dear Amber,

We're out to sea a week now, and is it ever awesome. Nothing but dark blue ocean and gray sky. Seagulls followed us for two days, then flew away. I miss their sounds. Out here there's nothing but the sound of water, not a speck of land In any direction. This morning, the sun's come out, and it sure looks good. I can hardly wait until we get to Africa.

BTW, regular e-mailing is tough. The captain rations the time any one person can be on the special hookup, so I promise to write a long letter and mail it when I can. I'm so busy during the day that by nighttime, I just fall into bed and pass out.

My roomie, Ingrid, is truly cool! This is her second trip on the ship, so she's a real source of info for me. We're in the galley (that's the kitchen) together. Can you imagine me cooking? It's true. I can do scrambled eggs for almost two hundred in no time!

Most evenings, after all our chores are done, a bunch of us sit on deck and talk. The kids on board come from all over, and they're MAJORLY interesting. Plus, they're really knowledgable. They talk about world events like TV newscasters. They have opinions and ideas. I think of my friends at home who may know the hottest fashion trends but can't tell you what's going on politically in Bosnia, and I'm embarrassed. Yikes, did I just call my friends shallow? (Sorry.)

Miguel (he's from Madrid) has a guitar and after we finish talking and solving the world's problems, we sing while the stars twinkle down. I can hear the waves slapping against the hull of the ship and everything is so peaceful, it makes me want to cry with happiness. I've never been happier. And I haven't even gotten to the REAL work in Africa yet!

Hate to cut this short, but others are waiting in line for the modem plug. So, hang in there and try not to have too much fun without me. Hugs to Mom and Dad.

Heather hit Send and stared thoughtfully at the screen. She thought of all the things she hadn't written. She hadn't mentioned Ian. In other e-mails, she'd told Amber about meeting him, and about how cute she thought he was, but she hadn't confessed just how much she was liking him. No matter how long her day or how tired she felt, her spirits soared whenever she was around him. She couldn't call it a crush exactly—she'd had crushes on guys back in high school, so she knew what a sweaty-palms, racing-heart crush was like. This was different because *he* was different. She could hardly explain it to herself, much less to her sister.

Heather sighed and unplugged her laptop. She told herself that maybe she should give up sitting on the deck in the moonlight talking and listening to Miguel play the guitar. Maybe it would be best to turn in early rather than talking into the late hours of the night. Maybe staying away from Ian was the best thing to do.

She stood and shook her head decidedly. Then again, maybe it wasn't.

Each Monday and Wednesday morning, Heather met in the ship's conference room with Dr. Henry, the coordinator for her group, and the fifteen others assigned to the inland mission team. Dr. Henry, a surgeon and internist from Boston, stood six foot three and made a dramatic first impression. He was in his fifties, wore round, dark-rimmed glasses, and had a head of thick white hair. He was a veteran of the Mercy Ship and of Ugandan expeditions, telling the group that this was his tenth trip aboard the ship in twenty years.

"Uganda is a country that's been heavily influenced by the British," Dr. Henry said in his first lecture. "In fact, English is the 'official' language of the country, although you'll hear a lot of Swahili and Lugandan. Swahili has been spoken for over a thousand years in Africa, so it's good to know some words and phrases.

"When you meet an African, it's customary to open with *'Habari,'* which means 'What news?' And the standard reply is *'Mzuri,'* 'Good.' This formality is considered good manners, so try and remember to follow their protocol. All right, let's practice."

The group repeated the words, memorizing the inflections. *"Mzuri,"* Dr. Henry said with a smile. "Another plus is that most Ugandans are literate. The best schools have waiting lists and are connected with the Anglican Church. The British influence in Uganda carried over into their schools. Children are sent off to boarding schools when they turn six. They live on campus year-round, partly because the roads within the country are so poor that it's impossible for children to return home daily. Kids have three traditional holidays a year. Formal education ceases in the seventh grade, but the brightest go on to upper-level schools. University abroad is for but a chosen few."

Heather knew two girls who'd gone away to private boarding schools, but each of them had a car and could come home when she wanted. Heather tried to imagine being a first-grader and not coming home from school every day. Or being cut off from her family for an entire school term.

Because Heather was to become a hospital aide, she also participated in basic first-aid courses, including CPR and trauma training. "Safety first," Dr. Henry told his team. "Double-glove at all times, especially when coming in contact with patients' body fluids. I know each of you has had basic inoculations, but we can't inoculate against HIV, so always be careful."

Before leaving the States, Heather had received an armful of vaccines, as well as a shot of gamma globulin to boost her immune system. She was taking typhoid and malaria medications by mouth daily. Her parents also had insisted that she carry a package of syringes in her luggage. Her father had said, "Medical supplies are at a premium in these countries. It isn't unusual for syringes to be reused, which runs a risk of contamination from other illnesses. Let's hope you don't need them, and when you leave, you can donate any of your leftover supplies to the hospital."

During a break, Heather turned to Patrick, a student of Dr. Henry's and an Ugandan. He had participated in their late-night gabfests. "Glad to be going home?"

"Yes. I have not seen my family for three years."

"Really? How come?"

He smiled. "It is a long way. And my father is not a rich man."

Of course. Why had she asked such a dumb question?

"My father is a teacher," Patrick said. "He has many children but only one wife." He laughed heartily, as if he'd made a hilarious joke. Heather didn't get it. "Because he teaches children, he has many," Patrick supplied, as if hoping she might finally catch on.

"One wife? Has he been married before?" That was the part that baffled Heather.

"In my country men take more than one wife," Patrick explained. "It is not unusual for a man to have two or three wives and ten, maybe fifteen children."

"But aren't there laws? Rules about bigamy?"

Patrick shook his head. "No. And that is one thing the Christian church is trying to change."

"I should think so."

Patrick regarded her with intense brown eyes. "Not for the reasons you may think. A man usually has only a small farm to grow food and make a living. If he has several wives and many children, how will he leave a proper inheritance when he dies? So then, the children are fighting over an acre of land. This is not good, brother against brother, woman against woman. The ground in Uganda is very rich, but how can an acre support a family of twenty when each is claiming a portion as his inheritance?"

"So if a man only has one wife, then he can pass his property down more efficiently," Heather said. "I understand." Patrick's logic was simple, but Heather was shocked to think of its being acceptable for a man to take several wives. Yet Patrick acted as if it were nothing extraordinary.

"This is true. And also, can you picture living in a house with many women, each thinking she is the best wife?" His expression was one of mock horror. "What man can stand the pressure? He might go off and meet another woman and marry her!"

She laughed.

Patrick sobered. "But there is even a far more serious problem with taking many wives. In my country, the HIV virus is spreading like a fire on the Serengeti. Dr. Henry will tell you, one in three Africans test positive for HIV. It is true. And when a man sleeps with many women, the virus is spread even faster. So my father keeps just one wife."

Heather had heard the lectures in school—unprotected sex and IV drug use were among the primary causes of the spread of HIV. Now she was hearing it again from a young man whose entire country was at risk. She looked into Patrick's eyes and said, "Your father's a very smart man."

"And my mother is a very jealous woman," he said with an impish wink.

One of the things Heather missed most of all was seeing green grass and bright, tropical flowers. The ocean world was beautiful, but the vast sea of blue sometimes depressed her. And some days, in spite of the bright sun, the sea air was cold. She stepped out on deck one morning to brilliant sunshine, but a northwest wind blew along the length of the deck, making her shiver.

"Would you like my sweater, Heather?"

Ian stepped up beside her. He wore a cream-colored cable-knit sweater of Irish wool, and his hair looked windblown.

"Thanks, but I'm headed down to the galley, and it's nice and warm down there. We're baking bread today. Maybe some pizzas too—food of the gods."

Ian laughed and rubbed her arms briskly. "That's a strange dish."

"You don't like pizza? That's un-American."

"I'm a Scotsman, remember."

She dropped her head dramatically onto his shoulder. "Of course you are."

"If it's bread you like, you'd better eat your fill on the ship, because Ugandans have no equivalent."

"What? A land with no bread? What do they eat instead?"

"Rice. *Matoke.* That's a cooked plantain, a kind of banana." She made a face. He added, "It's served in a mushy pile, like potatoes, but it doesn't taste like potatoes."

"Oh, the hardship of service." Heather placed the back of her hand against her forehead and pretended to swoon. "Well, you can't scare me. I'm still going to Africa—with or without my daily bread."

Ian laughed heartily. "Your enthusiasm is noted. And you will need it once we get there. When the power goes down and there's no hot water to bathe yourself or the patients, you may feel different."

Heather bristled. "I can take a little hardship. I'm not made of glass, you know."

"I'm certain that's true. But I don't want you to get discouraged."

"Then why are you trying to discourage me?"

His expression grew serious. "Because I don't want anything bad to happen to you. And I'm not just talking about your safety. Sometimes the dreams we hold in our hearts don't always measure up to what we must face in our life."

"You're afraid I'll become disillusioned? You sound like my parents."

"Is that who I remind you of? Your father?" He pulled back, pretending to be horrified. "I would hate for you to think of me as your kin."

"Then stop treating me like a baby sister."

His smile turned soft. "I have a sister, Heather. I don't need another one."

She gave him a grudging smile, not certain what to make of his teasing. Did he like her? Or was he just worried that she might weaken the team because of her inexperience? She was prepared to sacrifice her personal comfort. She knew her time of service in Africa wasn't going to be a picnic. She said, "Well, I feel sorry for your sister because you probably watch over her like a hawk and criticize every guy she brings home. You should give her the benefit of the doubt. She just *may* know what she's doing."

"Yes, maybe that's so."

Heather knew they weren't really talking about his sister, but it seemed the best way to get her point across. "Now, I've got to get down to the galley, or you'll be begging for your lunch and it won't be there."

"Then I'll see you later."

Neither of them moved. They stood looking into each other's eyes while Heather's heart hammered. Ian reached out and softly ran the back of his hand along her cheek. She shivered, but this time it didn't come from being cold.

4

Dear Heather,

I could go on about how boring it is around here without you this summer, but why put you to sleep? Mom and Dad are so busy that they hardly ever come home—except at night when I have something else to do! Anyway, we don't see much of each other (their loss). I print out your e-mails and stick them onto the fridge so they won't go snooping on the computer. That way if you ever want to tell me something personal and private, I can edit it out before I print it for general consumption. Smart, huh?

The only daytime company I have is Mrs. Lopez, who at least takes care of food for me (or I'd starve!), and the gardeners. There's a really cute guy trimming the hedges as I look out the window. Oh, BTW, I put a 2-inch blond streak in my hair. My friends think it looks cool. Mom says I look like Cruella in "101 Dalmatians." This from a woman who hasn't changed her hairstyle in 20 years!

One bright spot to report. Last Thursday, I came out of the mall to a flat tire on my car. (That's not the bright part.) I was freaking, when Dylan Simms came up to me. You remember him? He's on the basketball team and he's going to be a senior like me in the fall. Surprise! He's really cute—how did I fail to notice until now? Plus, we have something else in common— we both think I'm adorable.

Honest! He's had a crush on me for almost a year. Good timing, huh? I mean, nothing else is going on, so I might as well have a fling with a new guy. And BTW, I don't care what you say about you and Ian. I can read between the lines, and I know when my sister's got the hots for someone. Besides, what's more romantic than to be out on the high seas with a dreamy guy?

Well, got to run. Dylan's taking me to a movie.

Amber (who's tan and thin and looks like a goddess, or almost)

A pang of homesickness stabbed at Heather as she read Amber's e-mail. She pictured the screened-in pool and her sister stretched out on her hot pink bubble raft, floating lazily in the middle. Amber would have a soda can propped in the raft's cup holder. She'd be reading a hot, sexy novel and listening to music blasting from the poolside speakers. They'd followed this routine together for years growing up.

But Miami was more than two thousand miles away from the tip of Africa. The *Anastasis* had sailed around the Cape of Good Hope two days before and was now on the final leg of the journey. Soon the Great White Ship would anchor off the coast of Kenya and Heather would be bused into Nairobi airport, then flown to Entebbe, Uganda, with the rest of her team. If only she could communicate the grandness of her adventure to Amber. But she couldn't.

She closed her laptop with a sigh. Amber was right about one thing, however: Heather did have a thing for Ian. The more they talked, the better she got to know him, the more she liked him. But she wasn't going to let him see that. She hadn't come on this trip to have a romance. She'd come to help people have a higher quality of life. This trip wasn't about her, but others. Ian understood the concept perfectly. Amber might never get it.

* * *

One afternoon, Heather wandered into the refurbished lounge where school was held for the children of the crew and staff. Tables, desks, computers, and student artwork made the room look overstuffed. She found Mrs. Hoover, the teacher, busy scrubbing modeling clay off desks. "Can I help?" Heather asked.

The small, dark-haired woman straightened and flashed a tired smile. "Absolutely. What was I thinking to let them have clay and finger paints on the same day?"

Heather picked up a wet sponge from the bucket on the floor and set to work on a desk. "How many kids are on board?"

"Twenty—and a half, if you count Melissa Vanderhousen, who's due to give birth this fall." She chuckled. "But only fourteen come to school. The rest are too young."

"But you teach all of them? Even though they're different ages?"

"Yes, it's a real zoo some days."

"How do you do it?"

"Independent study for the most part, some group activities. And the older ones help the younger ones." Mrs. Hoover looked up. "You're Heather, aren't you? I'm Barbara. My husband, Bob, is in charge of the construction crew going into Uganda. Our kids and I will stay here on the ship."

Heather liked Bob Hoover and told Barbara so. "You know, I can't remember a time I haven't wanted to do this. How about you? It doesn't seem easy to uproot a family and stick them on a ship in the middle of the ocean." The trip was an adventure for Heather, but she knew it must be harder for families.

Barbara paused. "Actually, it was easier than I thought it would be. Four years ago, we lived in Atlanta. Bob was a partner in a large engineering firm. I was a teacher at a junior college. We had a gorgeous house, two cars, plenty of money in the bank. We were respected pillars of our church in the suburbs, and"—she paused—"we weren't happy. On the surface, we had it all. But in our hearts, frustration.

"The crowning blow came when our oldest, Todd, came home from school one day and announced that he wanted these sneakers that cost a hundred and fifty dollars. I told him no, and he pitched a fit. He was nine years old and ranting about sneakers that cost enough to feed a small country. That very night, Bob and I sat down and reevaluated our priorities."

Barbara dipped her sponge into the bucket and squeezed it out. "As timing would have it, that weekend missionaries came to our church and talked about their service aboard a Mercy Ship in the Caribbean. My husband and I looked at each other, and we knew what we wanted to do. We sold off most of our worldly possessions, and within nine months we were aboard this ship. It's been almost a year now."

She straightened. "We're the winners, you know. I've seen my kids become better for it. Without television every night, they read, they play with kids from many other countries, they've learned foreign languages. In short, they have an appreciation for life they never would have had back in Atlanta.

"As for Bob and me, we don't miss the rat race one bit. Some of our friends back home think we're crazy, but who cares? I've shopped in ports of call from Europe to Africa. Bob's helped build housing for some of the poorest countries in the world. We've traveled to the most interesting places. We love it. And you know what the Bible says." She didn't wait for Heather to answer. "It says that we must be doers of the Word, not only hearers." She looked down at the smeared mess on the desk. "And I can assure you, dear, I'm a real doer today."

Heather thought about her parents, about their medical practice and their lifestyle. They still had social consciences and continued to perform plastic surgery for battered women and abused children. She was proud of them for that. "You know," she said to Barbara, "I have some free time on Thursday afternoons. Why don't I come help you?"

"That's kind of you, and much appreciated. You're on." Barbara stacked some books. "I know this lifestyle isn't for everybody. And before making such changes a person must always count the cost."

"What do you mean?"

"Because we're doing this, there are things our family won't ever do. We've wondered how it will affect our kids when they become adults. Will they follow in our footsteps, or will they reject this kind of life?"

Heather shook her head. "I never went anywhere like this when I was growing up, but my parents talked all the time about their service in the Peace Corps. It seemed so much more interesting to me than what my friends were doing—worrying about who liked who, and stuff like that. My sister, she's different. I don't think she'd ever do anything like this. Not enough creature comforts."

Heather caught herself and reddened. "Not

that Amber isn't terrific. She'd do anything for a friend. But this sort of thing, taking care of people she doesn't know, well, it's just not her."

Barbara gave Heather a sharp look, then said, "We're not humanitarians, Heather. I've met many—United Nations workers, government relief workers. I know that the world has many good people who really care about serving their fellow man. But that's not why we do it. We do it because we want to see the Gospel spread all over the world."

She sounded like Ian. On a mission for a higher goal than simply healing people's bodies. Heather wondered again where she fit into the scheme of things.

"I'm sorry," Barbara said with a smile. "Here I am preaching to you and all you want to do is help me clean desks. I didn't mean to get carried away."

"No problem," Heather said lightly. But there was a problem. She knew she didn't feel the same kind of fire that the Hoovers and Ian felt. She was motivated, but not in the same way, not by the same force. Perhaps in Uganda she'd find such a fire. But for now, she was just going along to help—because children were dying and she was young and strong and committed to changing things for them. If God wanted something else from her, then perhaps, somewhere along the way, he'd let her know.

The *Anastasis* sailed northward toward Kenya, still too far from land to see either the island of Madagascar to the east or Mozambique on the African mainland to the west. The moon made a bright white trail on the calm waters of the Mozambique Channel as Heather relaxed in a deck chair, listening to Miguel singing in his beautiful tenor voice. Beside her, she heard Ian humming along, slightly off-key.

"Ian," she whispered, "why is there a ring around the moon?"

"Ice crystals," he answered. "Away up in the atmosphere."

"But it's not that cold."

"Remember, lass, you're below the equator now. It's winter."

"That's right. I forgot."

She felt his breath against her neck as he leaned toward her. "Did you see the sky this morning?"

"Sorry, it was dark when I headed for the mess hall."

"The sky was red."

"Meaning?"

"There is a saying from the sailors. 'Red sky at night, sailor's delight. Red sky in the morning, sailors take warning.' "

She turned to better see his face in the moonlight. He looked serious, all traces of teasing gone from his expression. "What are you telling me?"

"I read the bulletin that came over the navigator's telex. There's a storm coming. I fear we're in for quite a blow."

5

Pain woke Heather in the middle of the night. Tossed hard against the wall beside her bed, she seized hold of the bed rails to keep from being pitched to the floor. The cabin had turned cold and black.

"Ingrid!" she cried. "What's happening?"

"Storm," Ingrid said, after which Heather heard a thump and a yelp.

"Are you all right?"

"I hit my head."

Heather was disoriented—for a moment, she felt as if she'd been turned upside down. I—I think I'm going to be sick to my stomach."

"No! Try to sit up."

Terrified, Heather struggled upright. She swung her legs over the side of her bed. The floor met her, sending a jarring pain through her ankles and calves. She gasped and tried to remember emergency procedures.

"We should go topside," Ingrid said. "To the mess hall. It's worse here down below. My uncle owns a fishing boat and I've been in storms before. We'll have to climb and be quick about it."

Heather had no idea how they were going to make it. Their room was five levels below the top deck, in the interior of the ship. They'd have to weave their way down the narrow corridors and up many flights of ladder stairs. It was a long trek even when the ship was in perfectly calm waters. Heather swallowed her fear and groped toward Ingrid's bed. She took Ingrid's hand. "Come on."

The two of them started to the door, taking time only to tug on sweaters and sweatpants. The ship heaved and yawed, slamming Heather against the dresser. She cried out, and Ingrid groped for her arm. "Hold on to me."

In the corridor, emergency lighting glowed an eerie red beam. They merged into a group of their shipmates inching along the metal handrail. The smell of vomit made Heather gag.

A hand reached out to steady her. "Come along, follow us," Ian said.

Shaking, she eased in front of him, making sure that Ingrid got in front of her. "I'm scared, Ian."

"It's a good ship. She's come through storms before. We'll make it."

On the journey topside, they opened the doors and led others out into the serpentine of people, climbing ladders slowly, hanging on whenever the ship made an especially nasty heave or roll. It seemed like forever, but eventually they made it to the inside corridor leading to the giant ballroom that had been converted into the mess hall.

The air was chilling. Power was out, but a few flashlights and battery-powered lanterns broke the darkness inside the room. The wind howled, reminding Heather of a runaway freight train. She looked out the row of windows and cringed. The sea, white and boiling, sent plumes of spray crashing against the plexiglass. She froze, mesmerized. The ship was nine stories high and still the sea washed over the decks! She felt rooted to the floor, too terrified to move.

"Come this way. I've a spot for us." She felt Ian's arm around her waist.

He guided her and Ingrid around huddled groups of people to a place along an inside wall. Miguel was there, and so was Patrick. They covered the girls with blankets. Heather couldn't stop shaking. "Will we die?" she asked.

"No," Ian said, pulling her close to his side. "God will see us through. Have faith."

She struggled against the urge to vomit. "Wh-What if I get sick?"

"There's no shame in it. We have buckets; just ask for one."

She swallowed hard, forcing back her nausea. For certain, she didn't want to throw up all over Ian. "How long is this going to last?"

"The feeling in your stomach, or the storm?" he asked with gentle humor.

"It feels like I'm dying," she moaned into the blanket.

"No one's ever died of seasickness," he said.

"Are you sure?"

"Yes, lass."

Children cried and parents murmured to them in soothing voices from the surrounding dark. From somewhere, Heather heard a father quote from the Twenty-third Psalm. " 'Yea, though I walk through the valley of the shadow of death, I will fear no evil: for thou art with me. . . .' "

Heather gripped Ian's arm, and he tucked the blanket more tightly around them both, folding her closer, whispering in her ear, " 'Be strong and courageous. Do not be terrified; do not be discouraged, for the Lord your God will be with you wherever you go.' That's one of my favorite verses. I say it when I'm afraid. And it comforts me."

She couldn't imagine Ian ever being afraid of anything. "I've never been afraid this way until now. Not even when I was in a hurricane in Florida."

"Heather, the storm will pass. And the ship will weather it. We will get to Africa." He tipped her chin upward. "Talk to me. Tell me what inspired you to choose Africa from all the places in the world."

"I—I used to watch *National Geographic* specials on TV. I wanted to come for a visit, see all the wild animals. Then a few years ago, I read a book." Heather's voice trembled as she struggled to shift her thoughts away from her fear and the sick sensation in her stomach. "It was about Dr. Livingstone and his hunt for the source of the Nile."

"A Scotsman," Ian said with genuine pride. "He inspired a whole generation to come."

She nodded. "He came as a doctor and missionary. He fell in love with Africa and spent his whole life mapping it out. He never gave up, even when people in England ridiculed him. His story made me want to come even more."

"Many missionaries came to Africa in those days. It was a time of a great religious revival. Did you know that when those missionaries left Britain they packed all their worldly belongings in boxes six feet long, three feet wide, and two feet deep? The size of a coffin. That way, when they died—and most died within six months of coming—they could be shipped home for burial."

A chill went through her. "No. I didn't know that."

"Disease got them, mostly."

"How about you? How did you end up wanting to help in Africa?"

"My great-grandfather was a physician and a minister. And, like Livingstone, he chose Africa for his life's work. I read his journals and they made me want to go there too. That's why I keep a journal. It is not nearly so filled with hardships as his, but maybe one day it will inspire another generation of McCollums to do the same."

"Will you write about tonight?"

"Yes. And also of the bonny lass who shared it with me."

Ian could lift her spirits so easily. She cleared her throat. "What happened to your great-grandfather?"

"He served fifteen years in Africa as a doctor. He took a wife, the daughter of a British captain serving in Egypt. They had three children, and when they came of an age to be schooled, he sent his family home."

"Did he see them again?"

"That he did. He went home in 1916, caught influenza, and died in his wife's arms."

"He died of the flu?" She found it hard to believe.

"That flu epidemic killed over a million people. Remember, there were no antibiotics in those days."

She felt sorry for a family she'd never known, while her heart brimmed with emotion for Ian. He was six years older than she but a hundred years wiser. His heart was full of tenderness and compassion, and already she envied whoever would become his wife. "Did your father ever want to be a doctor?"

"No. But he is a minister. He's the vicar in a country parish. It's a small village and it's where I grew up. In the autumn, the heather stretches across the moor as far as your eye can see. And before the heather colors the moor, the lavender grows. Its scent hangs in the breeze like the breath of angels."

Her mental picture of rolling hills speckled with wildflowers under blue sky made the fierceness of the storm fade momentarily. "I'd like to see Scotland someday."

"And I'd like to see America."

Suddenly the ship dropped like a stone. Adults cried out and children shrieked. Heather stifled a scream and clung more tightly to Ian.

Hastily Miguel picked up his guitar and began playing "Kumbayah." Shaky voices joined in one by one, singing softly, " 'Someone's crying, Lord, Kumbayah. . . .' " And when the song was finished, Miguel played "How Great Thou Art," and they sang that. Hymn after hymn followed, voice after voice sang words of comfort while the storm raged outside.

It seemed like an eternity to her before the heaving of the ship lessened, before the waves no longer crashed against the windows and the howling wind died down. Slowly, as the storm grew less intense, exhaustion made Heather's eyelids droop. In the warmth of Ian's arms, she drifted in and out of sleep. She dreamed she wore a long, dark dress, high-necked and long-sleeved, and a bonnet of midnight blue. She saw Ian leaning against a wall, wearing an old-fashioned suit. He held a medical bag in one hand, a Bible in the other. The wall grew transparent, and she saw Amber sitting by the ship's pool in a bikini. Heather turned and saw her parents anxiously peering through the windows of the mess hall. Fearful they'd be washed overboard, she cried, "Watch out!" and woke with a start.

The cold gray light of morning filtered through the salt-smeared windows while the ship rolled from side to side like a cradle rocked by some giant's hand. All around her people were stretched out, covered with clothing and blankets, sleeping. Her first thought was, *I'm alive!*

The horrible queasiness was gone, and she realized that soon all these people would wake and need to eat. But eating was the last thing she felt like doing! She turned and saw that Ian was no longer beside her. As quietly as possible, she stood, tucking her blanket around the sleeping Ingrid, then threaded her way to the door. On deck, she was hit by a stiff, damp breeze and the briny smell of wild ocean. The world looked gray, heavy with thick fog. The deck was wet and slippery, strewn with seaweed and a few broken planks. Long strings of sea algae dangled from the railings like thick bands of rope. Carefully she edged closer to the rail to look over the side. The sea was listless now, as if tired from being driven by the wind.

"Not too close, lass," she heard Ian say through the mist. "Couldn't have you falling in, now. We'd never find you in this soup."

He emerged from the fog like a ghost.

"I'm not about to fall overboard," she told him. "I worked too hard last night to keep from dying of fright."

"You should be inside."

"I woke up and missed you," she confessed. "Where'd you go?"

"Up to the bridge. Most of the crew's been up all night, making sure we didn't wash overboard. We lost some deck chairs, and a mooring on one of the lifeboats broke loose, but they were able to secure it again. The captain says that according to the radar, the storm's well west of us now. All in all, we weathered it well."

Heather sagged with gratitude. "I'd hate to go through that ever again."

He hooked his arm around her shoulders. "Yes, thank God for bringing us through."

"I—I was so scared, Ian. Weren't you?"

"Yes. But if I had died, then this morning I would have waked in a far better place for having crossed over."

"Well, I'm not ready to 'cross over,' " she told him. "I've still got a lot of living to do."

He laughed as if she'd just told him a funny joke. "Lass, we don't choose when we get to cross over. God does. And for those who believe, it doesn't matter which side of time we live on. This side, we do God's work and spread his word to others, waiting for when he calls us home to heaven, where we will spend eternity with him. We lose our life in order to gain it."

Heather longed to share Ian's faith and self-assurance, but the storm had left her bruised and badly shaken. Until the previous night, it hadn't occurred to her that she could actually die—that all her plans and dreams, her very future, could have been swept away by the wind from an angry sea.

6

Hi, Sis—

I survived a storm at sea! I'm not kidding, it was the scariest thing I've ever lived through—waves as high as downtown buildings. Believe me, it's sure changed my take on the ocean! Back home, the beach is a cool place to spend the day, and waves are swoopy heaps of water to ride our rafts on. But out here, with nothing but a few tons of metal between me and the bottom of the sea, I saw the ocean in a whole new light. It's strong and violent. And nothing can tame it. It makes a person feel helpless and insignificant. And it's made me wonder why people ever wandered off dry land in the first place.

It also makes me glad that I'm flying home straight from Uganda and not sailing again on the ship. One thing's for sure, I DON'T want to become fish bait!

BTW, the storm also set us back a few days. Now we're not due to reach Kenya until the first of the week, so there's been a little change in plans. Evidently, planes don't fly in and out of Nairobi each and every day. We have to wait until Thursday to fly into the airport in Uganda. That means me and the rest of Dr. Henry's team will help for a few days at a special World Health Organization project about half a day's drive from Nairobi. We'll be taken in buses to the compound, where Dr. Henry's told me that hundreds of people are already gathering for medical help. He says some of these people have walked for days, even weeks to be there when the doctors from the Great White Ship come to treat them. The worst cases will be bused back to the ship.

Ian tells me that it can get pretty crazy, and that I should be prepared to see some awful sights, diseases, open sores, malnourished kids. I've told him that I can take it, that I'm familiar with gross medical things. Honestly, he worries about me and it isn't necessary. I can do this, Amber. I can make a difference!

Heather signed off after reminding Amber that this would be her last chance to e-mail until she reached Uganda. She wished it weren't so, because she didn't like feeling totally cut off from her family and everything familiar. Still, she was glad to finally be getting to do the work that she'd come so far to do.

The storm had left a mess that had to be cleaned away before the boat docked. The ORs needed special attention, and it seemed to Heather as if she would never get out of the galley. She'd spent long hours packing the food and other supplies her group would need for the days they were to stay at the World Health Organization compound. She entered the galley, asking, "What's cooking?"

"Rice," Ingrid answered. A huge pot simmered on the stove.

Heather made a face. She was sick of rice and longed for a helping of french fries. "Yummy," she said without enthusiasm.

Ingrid laughed. "There's dried herring, too."

"Double yummy."

"I'd kill for a peanut butter and jelly sandwich," a boy named Boyce said. He was from Alabama, and his heavily accented Southernisms usually sent Ingrid into fits of giggles. As for Boyce, he'd taken one look at the stately Scandinavian girl and proclaimed her "cuter than a sackful of puppies."

"I stashed a couple of jars in my backpack," Heather said.

"I stashed some myself," Boyce admitted. "But I ate it during the storm."

"You're kidding."

"I was nervous. Eating it made me think of home."

"Thinking of food turned me green," Heather said.

Boyce leaned on his elbows across the counter. "So, what do you want for one of your jars? How about an Alabama football sweatshirt?"

"Dream on. I'm not parting with my peanut butter."

Boyce dropped to his knees and folded his hands in supplication. "Please. Pretty please with sugar on it. I'll be your slave for a day."

She poked him playfully. "Not for anything."

He begged all the harder, making them laugh. Heather ignored him but later that day did send him a small container with a scoop of peanut butter inside. When she told Ian about it, he said, "Yes, it's hard to come by some of these Uganda things."

"Are there any grocery stores?" she asked. They were standing on deck, watching the sun set over the water. The evening sky was streaked with pastel colors, and a few puffy clouds had turned bright pink, as if they were blushing.

"There are some small stores, but without refrigeration there's little that can be kept except what can be housed on the shelves in boxes and in cans."

"Where do the people get their food? Their fresh food, I mean?"

"They grow it. It's said that if you poke a stick in the ground, it'll sprout; the soil's that rich. And the wealthier people, they own cows and chickens. A man who has many cows is very rich indeed."

"I have no cows. Does that mean I'm poor in their eyes?"

He laughed. "You are an American. They believe all Americans are rich. But without a cow, what man will ever marry you?" His eyes danced mischievously. "A dowry of cows can get you a husband, you know."

"Is that the way a girl gets engaged? Her family arranges it with cows?"

"Sometimes. But men and women fall in love and get married without its being pre-arranged. Television has shown them the way we do things in the West, and so they want to follow in our ways. Yet tribal customs still remain. A man's tribe is his pride."

"His tribe?"

"In Africa, it matters which kingdom or tribe a person belongs to. It is a source of much fighting in this country. One tribe hates another. They go to war and many die. It's one of the things the church is trying to change.

To help men see each other as brothers in God's eyes.

"In Kampala, on Kasubi Hill, is the palace tomb of the kings of the Buganda Kingdom, still maintained and guarded by the Buganda clansmen. Their palaces are made of reeds and thatch, not like the palaces of the kings of Europe. You must remove your shoes, though, for it is sacred ground."

The ancient African world seemed mysterious and exotic, and it captured Heather's imagination. "Will you take me there? I'd love to see it," she said.

He sighed. "If there's time. There will be much to do, and we haven't much time."

"We have plenty of time," she chided. "Four whole months."

He smiled and brushed a wisp of hair away from her face. "It will pass in the twinkling of an eye. But we will be together, and that will make it happier for me."

"I like being with you, too," she said, feeling warm all over. "Even if we are from different tribes and I have no cows."

His laugh sounded rich and full. He hugged her shoulders. "Lass, you're a wonder. A blessing from the Lord. I will never forget you."

And then and there, she decided she would never let him.

Two days later, she saw her first glimpse of the Kenyan coast. "Look!" she cried, pointing to the west. "There it is!"

Ingrid and Boyce, who were with her swabbing down a deck, dropped their mops, and all three of them hurried to the railing. "That's it, all right," Boyce whooped. "We have arrived!"

"Not quite," Ingrid said in her practical way. "Two more days, I'd say."

Boyce hooked his arms through the girls' and together they stared out to the land rising on the edge of the sea. "My feet are begging to hit solid land."

"Mine, too," Heather said. Her lifelong dream of going off to other lands was coming true. She was more than five thousand miles from the sun-kissed shores of Miami, far from America and her way of life. All the plans, all the effort, all the work was about to pay off for her. And as a bonus she had never expected, she'd met Ian. Life didn't get any better than this!

7

Dust. In her hair, in her mouth, in her nose, in her very pores. Heather was choking on dust. She'd been in Kenya two days but had barely had time to do anything more than help unload supplies and food from the ship and reload it all into two decrepit buses, two vans, and a Jeep. On the third day, the convoy pulled away from the dock, away from the Great White Ship and through the city of Nairobi toward their destination, a World Health Organization facility a hundred kilometers to the north—into the grasslands, and into clouds of clinging red dust.

They left paved roads behind in the city and struck out on rutted dirt roads that jarred her teeth and kept her from taking a much-needed nap. The grasslands were flat and yellow with wild grass, broken only by an occasional gnarled tree. Far in the distance, she saw a range of mountains, but the mountains never seemed to get any closer, no matter how far the group traveled.

"How're you doing?" Ian asked, squeezing into the bus seat beside her.

"I think this is worse than the storm," she said, half shouting over the noise of the engine and the voices of the others. "Are my teeth loose?" She bared them, making him laugh.

"They look fine."

"Hey, I thought it was winter here. How come I'm sweating?"

"It's cooler at night. It's really quite pleasant, you know. In the summer it's over a hundred degrees."

"No complaints," she said, throwing up her hands. "I'm here, and I can't wait to get started."

He gave her an amused look. "You can't be faulted for lack of enthusiasm, lass. But get some rest if you can. We'll be there in a few hours, and then there'll be no time for resting. No time for anything except seeing the sick."

To oblige him, and because she was exhausted, Heather closed her eyes. The bus hit a pothole and tossed her hard into Ian's shoulder. She yelped. He caught her. Silently they stared into each other's faces. No need to

apologize. No need to say anything. He stead-
ied her, then returned to the back of the bus.

The WHO compound rose out of the flat
land like an old-time fort. Several portable
buildings were clustered behind a tall wire
fence that stretched around a large open area,
with a gate made of wire and timber. Guards
dressed in military uniforms were positioned
at the gate. Heather didn't need to ask why
guards were needed. One look at the mass of
humanity camped around the gates explained
everything.

As they drove up, people surged forward,
surrounding the bus and forcing it to slow to a
crawl. Heather stared out at an ocean of dark
faces. Men crowded against the bus. Women
held up babies and small children, as if im-
ploring the workers to take them through the
windows.

"What do you think?" Boyce asked, leaning
across Heather to peer out the window. "Think
they're anxious to see us?"

"I—I've never seen anything like it," Heather answered, immediately consumed with pity
for the children.

"Then you've never been to a 'Bama game,"
Boyce joked, but Heather could see by the ex-

pression on his face that he was taken aback too. "Looks like half the country's showed up."

"How will we ever help all of them?" The bus inched forward. Packed along the fence were makeshift shelters of cardboard and other tattered material. Small cooking fires dotted the ground, and the smell of charcoal hung in the hot, sticky air.

"We've got four days to find out," Boyce said. "Then it's off to Nairobi airport and on to Uganda."

Ian's words came back to her. How would they ever take care of so many people in such a short time?

By now, the convoy was through the gates and parked inside the compound, where order prevailed. Heather stood, slapped the dust off her arms, and filed off the bus with her group. Dr. Henry led them inside a small building adjoining a larger one. There they were greeted by a Dr. Greeley from England. He shook hands with Dr. Henry, then turned to the new arrivals.

"Welcome," he announced in a booming, rapid-fire voice. "As you can see, we've got our hands full. A few of the peacekeeping soldiers will help offload supplies, and nurses will direct their disposal. The OR schedule is already full for the day, but we will need some of you to help organize tomorrow's group. It's important that each patient understand that they can't eat or drink eight hours prior to their surgeries. Interpreters are available.

"The mess hall is the building on your right. We have a small refrigerator because we have our own generators. We store vaccines and medications in it, so it's off limits for anything else. There are bottled and boiled water available too. Those of you on construction, follow Private Luswa. We need more latrines dug."

Heather stood wide-eyed. She had thought she'd have more time to get instruction, more time to become acclimated to the hurly-burly, circuslike atmosphere.

"This way," Ingrid said, taking hold of Heather's arm. "We'd better get our tents up, because once it's time to go to bed, you're going to want to pass out. We'll come back for our assignments."

Heather followed her friend to the housing area. One-person canvas tents sat in orderly rows, looking to Heather like a Boy Scout farm. Quickly she found her gear in the pile already stacked by the soldiers. At boot camp, she'd learned how to erect a one-person tent and bed down in it. Now, in the wilds of Kenya, the tent would be her home.

Beyond the tent city, she saw rows of portable toilets, where the construction crew was already digging a long, narrow pit to accommodate the new arrivals. Attached to the outside of another building were outdoor showers with plastic walls just high enough to conceal a person's torso. A large tank hung over the unit, with open-ended pipes aimed downward.

"The tank collects rainwater," Ingrid said. "The sun heats it all day, so it is not too cold to bathe in."

Heather unrolled her tent and set to work adjusting the center pole and hammering the stakes into the hard ground. Inside the tent, she rolled out her sleeping bag and squeezed her two duffel bags to one side. She had stuffed everything she could into the bags, making them almost too heavy to lift. Her laptop was wedged safely inside, but it was useless without a place to plug it in. She itched to read her e-mail, longing to hear news of home and to tell Amber everything that had happened since the storm.

As soon as their things were stashed, Heather and Ingrid returned to the main building, where the clinic was operating at full capacity. A nurse directed Heather to a long line of women and children whom another nurse, Josie, was interviewing.

"Hello, luv," Josie said in a British accent. "This is the screening area. I'll need you to take a history, then send them over there"—she pointed—"where they'll be examined by a physician. These are the less serious cases— scabies, bronchitis, diarrhea . . ." she rattled off a list of ailments.

"We give out antibiotics and inoculations and make very sure the mothers understand how the medications are to be given. Sometimes they give it all at once instead of over the days prescribed, which, of course, brings on a new set of problems."

Heather nodded, feeling nervous. She wanted to do a good job, but it looked overwhelming. The line stretched outside the door, seemingly endless, while mothers juggled sick and crying children with resignation. She couldn't even guess at the children's ages, but many were just tiny babies. She set about taking names and filling in forms, surprised at the number who bore familiar names, such as Harriet, Joseph, Ruth, and Michael. She could not even begin to spell their African names, but many of them helped her, for most were literate. They seemed like gentle people, stoic about the long wait, even jovial when talking among themselves.

She was also surprised at how young they were. Girls of fifteen and sixteen were mothers, and women who told her they were in their thirties looked worn out, as if their lives had been too heavy for them. She thought about her parents' patients, who came in for expensive cosmetic procedures to keep them looking young. Here, getting fed was the focus of everyday life.

Heather had no idea how long she stood taking down information, but when she finally took a water break, she noticed shadows encroaching across the floor. Evening was near, and the end of the line of people could be seen, cut off at the gate, hours earlier, by the soldiers.

"That's it for the day," Josie said, still cheerful, when the last woman and child stepped up. "You look exhausted, child. Do sit down before you fall over."

"Thank you." Gratefully Heather eased onto a wooden bench. Her legs ached from standing, and her fingers were cramped from writing. "Is that it for today?"

"For today," Josie said. "It will begin anew tomorrow."

"How'd we do?"

"The doctor saw one hundred and fifteen patients." Josie smiled broadly. "And most were treatable."

Startled, Heather asked, "Most? Which ones weren't?" She racked her memory, trying to conjure up the faces of those who had passed in front of her. There had been so many.

"Two babies were placed in our hospital ward. Dysentery has left them barely alive."

How could that be? Heather had seen each child with her own eyes. How could she have not been sensitive to the few who were so critically ill they had to be hospitalized? "Will they be all right?"

"Hard to say, luv. You know, the baby gets sick in the village, the mother walks for days to get here, they wait outside for a turn . . . by then the child is pretty far gone. We put them on IVs to replace the fluid, but it's often too late."

"Gosh, I'm sorry. Poor little babies."

Josie patted her hand. "Brace up, dearie. We can't save them all."

Josie came across as almost flippant, and Heather hoped she herself would never grow indifferent to the suffering.

"Run along, now," Josie said. "You should be

having your dinner, then to bed. Lots more to do on the morrow."

Outside, night was falling and the temperature had dipped. Heather glanced toward the mess hall, lit by electricity, fueled by gas generators. The smell of charcoal fires from the encampment filled the air, and stars were winking on. That night she would fulfill a childhood dream—she would sleep beneath the skies of Africa.

From somewhere in the outer darkness, a baby cried. Heather shivered, then hurried toward the lighted building, toward a warm meal, toward the company of friends.

8

Heather woke in the middle of the night, and in spite of her bone-deep exhaustion, she couldn't go back to sleep. Gone were the familiar drone of the ship's engines and the squeak of metal plates and bolts. In their place, she heard the faraway howls and yips of night-hunting wild animals, which sent shivers up her spine. And she heard the forlorn crying of babies from the camp outside. She kept thinking about them, the babies and children too little and too sick to fend for themselves.

She thought about their sweet, round, dark faces when they'd come for treatment. Some had clung to their mothers. Others had simply stared out with blank expressions, seemingly resigned to whatever was going to happen. She realized that her house in Miami would seem palatial to most people. Her allowance alone could probably feed a family for weeks. Guilt stole over her. Guilt because she had so much, while these people had so little. But that was why she'd come, she reminded herself. To make a difference in other's lives. After all, wasn't she supposed to be God's hands on Earth?

She lifted the flap of her tent and stared out into the compound. The silhouettes of other tents hunkered down in the darkness. Overhead, a million stars glowed. The sight took her breath and lifted her spirits. Surely God was in his heaven and knew the suffering of the people. How could he turn an indifferent ear to them?

She remembered that she had packed hard candies in her bags. Tomorrow she would stuff handfuls in her pockets and give a piece to every child who passed through the clinic doors. She vowed to work twice as hard, twice as long. After all, she would be returning to Nairobi with her group in a few days. She'd have time to rest on the trip to Nairobi and on the plane ride to Uganda. Now it was time for work.

Out of the darkness, she heard the plaintive notes of Miguel's guitar. She followed the sound. Behind one of the buildings, she found Miguel, Boyce, and Ian sitting on the ground together. "Is this a private party?" she asked.

"We're praying," Ian explained. "Come join us."

She sat cross-legged on the ground beside him. "I didn't mean to interrupt."

"No problem," Boyce said. "Can't have enough prayers, can we?"

"Is there something you want to ask God for?" Ian wanted to know.

"Success," she said. "I guess that's what we all want, isn't it? I want the people who come here to get well."

Ian asked God to be merciful to those who were sick, and the rich sound of his voice comforted Heather. She'd never heard anybody pray with such devotion.

After the group broke up, Ian walked her back to the tent area. "That's me," she said, pointing. "Fifth row, fourth tent."

"I should have known. It's the prettiest tent of the lot."

She giggled. "It's dark and they all look alike."

"No, yours is different. Just because it's yours."

She felt a warmth spread through her. She looked at him, and by the light from the sliver of moon in the sky, she saw that he was watching her intently. For a moment she thought he might kiss her, and her heart pounded in anticipation. But he squeezed her hand and stepped away. "You should be in bed. Tomorrow will come quickly."

Disappointed, she nodded. "Thanks for letting me join you tonight. It was good to have all of us together again."

"You can join us anytime. We will meet to pray every night when things quiet down." He turned, then paused. "Are you making a difference, Heather? I know how much you wanted that for yourself."

"Not yet. But I've only just begun."

He smiled. "Yes. You've only just begun."

She watched him walk away, wondering what was going on in his mind. Wondering if he ever thought about her as anything other than just some idealistic high-school girl. Wondering if she could ever find a place in his heart.

By midday, she had almost lost her resolve of the night before to work twice as hard. Heat seeped like steam from a hot faucet through the metal walls of the hut used for a treatment room. Heather mopped her forehead and tried to tune out the sounds of people in pain. Today she was doing more than taking histories. She was assisting two nurses as they dressed a young woman's wounds. The woman had fallen off a truck, had gotten her foot caught, and had been dragged over hardened, rutted ground. Her ankle was badly sprained, and all the skin had been scraped off her back. Heather's stomach had lurched when she saw the pulverized flesh, but she'd fought off the nausea and quickly gathered the items the nurses needed.

"Sterile water," one nurse ordered.

"We're out," Heather answered.

"Go to the supply room and get two bags. And do hurry."

Grateful to get away from the pain-racked woman, Heather jogged to the next building, where supplies were kept in a locked room. Martha, an older woman who'd been with Heather on the ship, was responsible for the key. Heather told her what she needed, and Martha entered the room, emerging minutes later with two clear, plump fluid-filled bags. "Supplies are dwindling."

"Already?"

"They go fast when there are so many to use them."

Heather was dismayed. The ship had spent weeks taking on donated supplies in London. "When I get home, I'm going to do a fund-raiser for the ship," she announced firmly. "My parents' friends have wads of money. They can donate some of it to help buy medical supplies. I'll make sure they do."

Martha grinned. "That's the spirit. I can't imagine any of them refusing you."

"They better not." Heather knew she could persuade these wealthy people to give money to the cause. She'd work on a community fund-raiser too. Maybe she could get coverage in the newspaper and on TV.

Excited by her idea, she rushed back to the treatment room. But when she arrived, the atmosphere had grown chaotic. A child, badly burned from a fall into an open cooking fire, had been brought in. "Best to take a break," one of the nurses told Heather, taking the water from her as she stepped inside the door.

The child was screaming, and two other nurses were busy helping one of the doctors hold him down. His anxious mother hovered nearby.

Heather stepped back without argument. The child's cries were almost unbearable. She went to the mess hall, where she grabbed a bottle of drinking water. From there, she re-treated to the back of the compound, near the tents. Shaking, she leaned against a scrub tree and forced herself to breathe deeply. The doctor would help the child, she told herself. The child would be all right. She slid to the ground, bracing her spine against the tree.

Back home, a child with such burns would go into a special burn unit. Out here, there was no such thing. If he was in bad enough shape, they might take him into Nairobi to be hospitalized, but she could hardly imagine such a trip for a child already in agony from bad burns. She wished there were something she could do to help.

Someone shouted, *"Rafiki, rafiki!"*

Heather looked up to see a group of women and children gathered outside the fence not too far from where she was sitting. She acknowledged them with a wave.

"Rafiki," they called out again. *"Njoo!"* They beckoned to her.

Did they want her to come over to the fence? Heather glanced around, but there was no one else. "Me?" she asked.

"Njoo. Tafadhali."

She recognized the Swahili word for "please." Dr. Henry had taught the word to her group. Slowly she stood, and with her pulse racing, she edged to the wire fence. The women all talked at once. "I—I can't understand you," she said. "English?"

The women kept talking in Swahili.

"I—I'll go get someone—" Heather turned, but the group let out such cries that she turned back.

She heard a wail from the back of the group and saw an object wrapped in a piece of dirty cloth being lifted. It was passed quickly overhead, from woman to woman. Mesmerized, Heather watched, and as the bundle came steadily toward her, she caught a glimpse of a face. Suddenly she realized that the object was a baby, and that the women meant to pass it to her over the top of the fence. Except that the fence was eight feet high.

"No! No!" she cried, stepping away. "I'll get some help."

But the crowd ignored her. The baby, bundled in rags, continued to be passed. At the barrier, the last woman to take the baby hoisted it over the top. Heather ran back to the fence, frantically begging her not to drop the baby over. But there was no stopping the woman's momentum. Heather positioned herself to catch the baby.

Please, God, don't let me drop it, she pleaded silently.

Time passed in slow motion. The bundled baby balanced on the woman's fingertips, teetered, then tipped. Heather stood on tiptoe, reached up, and felt the infant slide into her outstretched hands. "Got it!" she cried. She eased it down, clutching it to her breast.

Her heart hammered and her arms and legs trembled, but she felt jubilant. The baby was safe in her arms. She felt it wriggle and heard it let out a weak cry.

She flashed a relieved smile at the women, but they had stepped back and were dispersing. "Wait!" Heather called. "Don't go! I need the mother. Who's the mother?" She racked her brain for the Swahili word for "mother" but couldn't remember it.

The women continued to melt away. Heather watched until only one very young woman was left standing far back from the fence. She stood tall and wore an expression of hopelessness. Then she, too, began to walk away.

"Wait!" Heather shouted. She watched as the woman picked up her pace and headed quickly away from the camp, off into the tall grass. Heather glanced down at the baby in her arms and pulled aside the tattered material covering the tiny face. The baby lay quite still. Its eyes were wide open, and its skin was the color of ash from a burned-out fire.

A cry rose in Heather's throat, strangled, and died on her lips.

The baby was dead.

9

In Heather's eighteen years of living, nothing had prepared her to look into the face of death. Not her education, not her upbringing, not her experiences, not any of her training for the Mercy Ship program. Nothing.

Death was final. Death was irrevocable. Life was flutterings and tremblings. It was warm breath and soft sighs. It was flesh that felt warm and didn't look waxy. In her arms, the dead baby felt almost weightless, as if its bones were hollow, like a bird's bones. Just minutes before, its lungs had filled with air and it had looked up into her face. Now those same eyes stared fixedly, their pupils dilated. They would never see again.

Heather began to shake, and despite the intensity of the noonday sun, she felt icy cold.

She didn't know what to do. She couldn't abandon the baby. She couldn't dig a hole, put the baby in it, and cover it over as she and Amber had done for their goldfish when they'd been kids. She couldn't go too far away, either. What if the mother returned? What if she wanted her child back?

Somehow Heather made it to the tree. She slid down the trunk and sat on the hard ground, carefully balancing the dead infant on her lap. And slowly she unwrapped the soiled cloth. The baby, a girl, lay naked within. Her belly looked distended, and her ribs bulged through her thin, dark skin. Heather counted each rib, running her finger along the ridges that no longer heaved with breath.

The tiny girl's forehead was wide and smooth as glass, and she had only the barest beginning of black fuzz covering her head. Her arms and legs were no bigger around than sticks—skin wrapped around hollow bones, Heather thought. The baby's face looked skeletal, like an old person's. She had no fat, round cheeks like those of other babies Heather had seen.

As she held the small body, Heather felt the infant's limbs growing rigid—rigor mortis was setting in. A fly buzzed past Heather's hand

and settled on the baby's cheek. "No!" Heather cried. "No. No. No." She quickly flipped the cloth over the little body and sent the fly whizzing away. Vermin would not take this child. No way. She'd see to that. Heather felt her shoulders heave. Her vision blurred as tears filled her eyes, and she wept as if her heart were breaking.

Heather didn't know how long she sat crying. She had no sense of time passing. But it must have passed, because the shadow of the tree grew longer over her, and her back and legs grew numb from not moving. She sensed someone coming up to her and crouching down. She didn't look, couldn't bear to look, because life had no rapport with death. And inside, Heather felt as dead as the child in her lap.

"Are you all right, lass?"

Ian. She didn't look at him, but she shook her head.

"People are asking for you. No one's seen you for hours. They're worried."

She couldn't find her voice.

"What have you there in your lap? Will you show me?"

She wanted to, but her fingers wouldn't move.

"Let me have a look-see." His fingers moved deftly to the edge of the cloth and gently pulled it aside.

She heard his breath catch. He was looking at the baby, at death, just as she had. Now he knew. He had seen. Finally she could answer him. "I don't know who she is. I never heard her name." Her voice sounded thick and foreign to her own ears.

"Can you tell me how you came by her?"

"They gave her to me. The women at the fence. They passed her over the top this noontime, and I caught her."

"And you've been sitting here alone with her all this time?"

"I couldn't let the flies land on her," Heather said matter-of-factly. "You understand, don't you?"

"We should be taking her to Dr. Henry. She should have a Christian burial."

"And flowers. She should have flowers, too."

"Come, Heather." Ian slid his arm around her waist and urged her to stand.

Her legs wouldn't work at first. He massaged her calves until a prickly sensation began to radiate through them. Then, with Heather pressed against his side and his hand cupping hers beneath the bundled baby, they walked slowly to the main building, while the long shadows of afternoon made dark, joyless smudges on the parched African earth.

"Whooping cough and dysentery would be my guess," Dr. Henry told Heather after he had examined the infant. "She didn't have much of a chance. Both are preventable, but her case was too far advanced. It's doubtful we could have saved her."

If his words were supposed to comfort Heather, they didn't. "Her mother left her. She left her with me, a stranger."

"She probably knew she was dying," the doctor said kindly. "You were her last hope."

"How could she do that? Just hand her over and walk away?"

"It was an act of desperation."

It was dark now, and the clinic had closed down for the night. The baby had been cleaned up and wrapped in plain white cloth, a shroud for burial. Ian had not left Heather's side since he'd found her.

Dr. Henry put his hand on Heather's shoulder. "Don't judge her harshly, Heather. People see death differently in other cultures. In America when a mother loses a child, we prescribe medications, she sees a grief counselor, maybe even a psychiatrist. There's a complete social service system to help her over her loss. But over here, these mothers can't afford to fall apart. They must get on with life quickly. Too many things are depending on them—food, care of other children, survival.

"Does that mean they don't grieve? Of course not. But in a country where the infant mortality rate is almost fifty percent, mothers have a different perspective on a baby's death. Some see it almost as a form of rescue from a harsh life."

"She shouldn't have left her," Heather murmured. "She shouldn't have."

Dr. Henry sighed. "You can't change what's happened. Please tell me, will you be able to continue with the work you came here to do? Because if you can't . . ."

Could she? Her lip trembled, but she said, "I can."

"Get some rest, then," Dr. Henry said. "Tomorrow the fight begins all over again. And, Heather, stay away from the fence. We have a system for patients to get into the facility for a reason."

Chastised, she nodded. She'd brought this on herself. "Will we have a funeral for her?"

"In the morning," Dr. Henry said. "Early."

Outside, Ian took her hand. "You haven't eaten all day. Let's get you some food."

"I can't eat."

"You can't let yourself get sick over this. It won't help."

"I'll be all right tomorrow," Heather said, without meaning it.

In the distance, she saw the glow of campfires lit by all the people still waiting to be treated. How long had some of them been there? Days? Weeks? How many had babies who wouldn't make it through the night?

"The first time I saw a person die, it affected me too, lass. Death is never an easy thing to accept. Doctors are supposed to chase death away. So we always feel defeated when it wins a round."

"I should have done something for her," Heather said quietly. "All afternoon, while I sat there with her, I kept thinking, *Why didn't I go get help sooner? Why didn't I grab the baby and run for help?* Maybe the doctors could have given her CPR. Maybe they could have gotten her breathing again. If I'd acted faster, maybe we could have saved her."

"You heard Dr. Henry say she was too far gone."

"He was trying to make me feel better."

"Heather, listen to me, you cannot let this defeat you."

"You tried to warn me, didn't you?"

"Warn you about what?"

"On the ship, every time we talked about my 'enthusiasm,' you tried to tell me that dreams and reality are two different things. You tried to tell me that we can't save everybody. I feel stupid. And I'm sorry I didn't listen to you." She thought back to the girl she'd been just a short time ago, when she'd first climbed aboard the Mercy Ship. Naive. Starry-eyed. Confident. So sure that she could make a positive contribution to the world. And today she had been powerless to get one tiny baby to medical help. So much for saving the world.

"I don't think you're stupid. And I think your dreams are good dreams. You cannot see yourself as a failure. We cannot come over here and heal every person who's ill. Why, we can't do that even in our own countries. We can only help one person at a time. And then another. And another. You *will* make a difference, Heather Barlow. Just maybe not in the way you once thought."

Ian could not take away the shame she felt, but his words had reached inside her and soothed the gnawing pain of self-doubt. She was grateful. "Thank you for being so nice to me."

He smiled tenderly. "It's not a hard thing to do, lass. We have months ahead of us on this trip. We have Uganda next and work there waiting for us. You cannot give up now."

Wrapping her arms around herself, Heather drew in a long shuddering breath. "I'm not giving up, Ian."

"That's the spirit."

No, she wasn't giving up. But she wasn't the same person she'd been when she'd first climbed aboard the ship. Or even the same one who had lain looking up at the stars the night before, believing that she was God's hands on Earth. Yesterday she had faced a long line of people whom she could help and had felt good about herself. Today she'd held a baby she could never help again. It had been life-changing.

"Will you come to the funeral with me?" she asked.

"Yes. I'll be there. And think on this, Heather. Perhaps at this very moment, that little one is in the arms of angels, near the throne of God. Could there be a better place for her to be?"

"No, I guess not."

"Then let her go in peace."

Before dawn the next morning, Heather gathered with her friends to pray and to watch Dr. Henry put the shroud-wrapped infant into the ground. "We are all saddened by the loss of this little one," Dr. Henry said to them. "We cannot understand why the Father has taken her home to be with him so soon. But take her he has. And all we can do is trust in his wisdom, which is far above ours. Let me read from Isaiah forty-one, verse ten:

'So do not fear, for I am with you;
do not be dismayed, for I am your God.
I will strengthen you and help you,
I will uphold you with my righteous right
    hand.'"

Heather felt Ian's hand slip into hers.

Dr. Henry continued. "This promise from God was given thousands of years ago, as a comfort to his people. And this next promise was given several thousand years later. I read now from Revelation twenty-one, verses three and four.

> '*Now the dwelling of God is with men, and he will live with them. They will be his people, and God himself will be with them and be their God. He will wipe every tear from their eyes. There will be no more death or mourning or crying or pain, for the old order of things has passed away.*' "

Dr. Henry closed his Bible. "I read these two passages because I want you to understand that God is faithful from age to age, and that his Word can be trusted. And now, *we* entrust the soul of this little one to the arms of a loving, faithful God. In the name of the Father, the Son, and the Holy Ghost."

In the silence that followed, Heather struggled against the lump clogging her throat. It was over. The baby was gone. Now dirt would fill the grave, and once it was trampled down, no one would know the hole's secret. For they had buried the baby deep to keep animals away once the facility was dismantled.

Heather had no flowers to give, but she had shaped a crude cross from a branch of the tree that had sheltered her and the baby the day before. She bent and placed it on top of the freshly turned soil. Then she stepped away. As the group dispersed, she watched the sun break over the horizon. It rose over the dry, grassy plain like a great orange ball, larger than a mountain, older than life itself.

10

The airport in Entebbe, Uganda, was less than an hour's flight from Nairobi, and from the air Uganda looked lush and green, different from Kenya's stark plains and grasslands. At the airport, Heather's group was met by two Ugandans sent by Paul Warring, the missionary in charge of the Kasana Children's Home. After they had cleared customs, the men drove them into Kampala, the capital. As they wove their way down the crowded streets, Heather was struck by the vivid contrasts between the rural and the modern in the teeming city.

Vans and late-model cars, high-rise buildings under construction, rows of shops and bazaars lined the streets, while cattle roamed the median strips along thoroughfares where makeshift tents and cardboard dwellings had been erected. The cattle, large, reddish brown animals with expansive horns, looked more like Texas longhorns than the docile milk cows she was familiar with and seemed oblivious to the noise of city life. "So those cows are what I need to find a good husband?" she asked Ian as she pointed out the window.

"Yes, there's your dowry."

"I guess I'll stay single, then. All Daddy has is cars."

He grinned. "That's a pity, lass."

"Do people really *live* on the median?"

"People live wherever they can. Kampala is home to a million Ugandans, most of whom have come to the city hoping to find a better life. But there's little work here, so they have nothing to do. They get up, grub for a day's living, sleep wherever they can."

The city didn't appear crowded. It was noon, and traffic flowed smoothly. In Miami, downtown would be filled with workers heading off to lunch, and traffic would be thick on the freeways. Here the people moved in no particular hurry. Many sat on benches or in front of stores, reading newspapers and sipping coffee. Most were dressed in Western clothing, but Heather saw several women wearing colorful Ugandan dresses and carrying large bundles balanced on their heads. Blaring radios poured sound through open shop doorways. She wondered how so many survived without jobs, how they got along from day to day.

The vans climbed up a winding, rutted road into hilly terrain. The sun shone brightly under a canopy of bright blue sky, and the air felt warm, but not steamy as it was in Miami. Banana trees and thick hedges, bright with exotic flowers, dotted the roadside, where the earth had a reddish hue.

"If I didn't know better, I'd swear I was back in my home in Alabama," Boyce drawled from a seat behind Heather's. "We have red dirt too."

The vans turned down a dusty road and pulled inside a compound surrounded by a low concrete wall. A large sign announced Namirembe Guest House. The L-shaped building was made of cinder block, painted white and bright blue, with a porch that ran its length. The vans parked and everyone piled out.

Ugandan women emerged from the building and greeted Dr. Henry warmly. He turned to his group and introduced the women as friends who would show them to their quarters. Once the vans were unloaded, Heather scooped up her bags and followed a woman named Ruth into a room that she would be sharing with Ingrid and two others, Cynthia and Debbie. The room's concrete floor was painted gray and the walls a pale green. A window with wooden shutters that could be closed at night let in warm sunlight. The beds were covered with clean sheets and old British army blankets. A wooden cross hung on one wall; a photo of an African Anglican bishop dressed in red robes hung on another.

Ruth pointed to a lone dresser and said, "You each have a bottle of boiled water. Use it for everything, even for brushing your teeth. The water closet is down the hall and turn right."

"Water closet?" Heather whispered to Ingrid.

"Bathroom," Ingrid whispered back.

"You should shower early because the water from the city is turned off every day to conserve, and sometimes it stays off for many hours. Hot water is scarce, so use it with care." Ruth smiled. "And there is water in buckets by the door you can use to flush the toilets when the water is off."

Heather had learned at boot camp about the primitive conditions she would face. She told herself that taking a warm shower and washing and blow-drying her hair every day were Western luxuries she'd willingly forgo in Uganda. It was a small price to pay for helping children who had never even seen the simple pleasures of life she and her friends took for granted.

"Dinner is from five until six o'clock in the dining hall," Ruth added. "And breakfast is served from seven until eight each morning. We wish that all of you have a pleasant and joyful stay at the guest house. I will help you, whatever your needs."

Once Ruth had gone, Cynthia said, "I'm crashing."

"Me too," echoed Debbie.

"I must write home," Ingrid announced. "Better to do it now."

Heather was in no mood to rest. She wanted to explore. She walked outside and took a stroll around the grounds, stopping at the perimeter wall to gaze down at the city below. She remembered Dr. Henry saying that once, Kampala had been pristine and beautiful— "the pearl of Africa." But after decades of military rule, it looked dingy and ruined. Heather heard a whooshing sound and turned to see two men cutting hedges and grass with long, thick-bladed machetes. Their swinging, singing blades glinted in the sunlight, mowing and pruning as machetes had done since ancient times.

"Beautiful, isn't it?" Ian asked, coming up beside her.

"Yes, it is. And it sure beats being blasted awake on a Saturday morning by a lawn mower." She closed her eyes and inhaled. The air smelled of freshly mown grass, tinged with lemon and charcoal.

"You smell lemon grass," Ian said. "It mingles with the scent of the charcoal cooking fires. It's a perfume that belongs only to the air of Africa."

She saw that his eyes wore a distant, longing look. "Do you like it as much as the smell of Scottish lavender?"

"A hard question, lass. Both are beautiful. Scotland is my home, but Africa has slipped inside my head and heart, and I have come to love it."

And she realized then that despite all that had happened to her in Kenya, she loved Africa too. "I'm glad I came," she said.

"Are you all right?"

Both of them knew what he was asking her about. "I still feel terrible about the baby," she said. "But I make myself think of something else whenever the bad thoughts come. I think about the look on the children's faces when I gave them candy after their shots. I think about how their smiles break out. I think about trying to make a difference in their lives."

She turned toward Ian. His red hair ruffled in the slight breeze. "On the road from the airport, I saw women walking with huge bundles on their heads," she said. "Some had babies strapped around their waists and little children following behind them. And I saw the cows walking around with only ropes around their necks to keep them from wandering off. And I wondered why the cows weren't carrying the bundles instead of the women. Why is that, Ian?"

A brightly colored bird landed on a tree branch and sent a shrill whistle into the sky.

"Perhaps you know the answer to that already, lass."

She nodded slowly. "It's because the animals have more value than the women, isn't it?"

"Maybe not more. But a different value, surely. Do not judge them for this difference, Heather. The animals are their livelihood, and a family without a cow has no milk to feed its children. Yet they want for their children what every parent wants—an easier life, a gentler way to take a living from the land."

Remembering what Patrick had told her on

the ship, she said, "I guess a man can get another wife, but another cow . . ." She let the sentence trail off.

"You can't measure their world by our standards. These people have lived for centuries with war, famine, pestilence, and death—the Four Horsemen of the Apocalypse in Revelation. In our countries, we believe we have conquered them, but we haven't. It's just that over here, we see them more clearly, more violently. That's what frightened you so in Kenya, Heather. You saw the baby in all its beauty. You saw death in all its ugliness. You saw how the two things do not go together, and it broke your heart."

She thought again about her parents, about how their medical skills went to fix people's physical imperfections and make them lovely once more. But people like Ian and Dr. Henry saw beyond the outside of a person. They saw with eyes of compassion to the inside, to the dark places. Places where hate and murder and sickness dwelled. Where the Four Horsemen wielded their swords as deftly as the workmen wielded their machetes on the grass.

She bit her lower lip. "I thought I could come and work and feel good about it and go back home and put this away in my scrapbook like I do other things in my life. But I don't think I can, Ian."

He grinned and touched her cheek. "That's the way it happened for me, too. I came once. It changed me. And now I come again. But this time, *you* have come."

"And that makes you happy?"

"Yes. Because you see Africa not only with your eyes, but with your heart. Coming here is not about bringing people medicine and supplies. It's not about doing good deeds for needy people. It's not even about taking a man's land and showing him how to plant it so that his crops grow tenfold. We do all these things, for sure. But that's not what it's all about."

He took a deep breath. "It's about changing lives. And the first life that changes is your own."

She couldn't deny anything he'd said. At the moment, all her reasons for coming seemed shallow and incomplete. They had been good reasons, but somewhere along the way, they had begun to grow roots. She didn't know how deep the roots would go. Nor did she know how she'd ever rip them out and return to the life she'd once lived.

* * *

On Saturday, Dr. Henry took a group into the city, and while he met with friends and church leaders, the group was free to wander. The first place Ian took Heather was Kampala's post office. "It's the only place that has a phone line outside the country," he explained. "If you want to call home, you'll have to wait in line along with all the other foreigners and make your call."

A foreigner. That was what Heather was in Africa. She hadn't thought of it that way before, until he'd said it. But she *was* a foreigner— one who wanted to hear her family's voices very much. "I feel like ET," she told him wearily after an hour's wait in line. "You know, I want to phone home, but I can't."

Ian grinned. "I know what you mean. And then if no one's home, it's a letdown. It's my father's habit to prepare his sermon for Sunday on Saturday, so I know he'll be in."

Heather wasn't sure anybody would be at her house, since it was seven hours earlier in Miami. Her heart sank as she realized that Amber was probably out. "Well, I don't care if all I get is the answering machine. I want to hear a familiar voice."

When it was finally her turn, Heather stepped into the old-fashioned wooden booth and closed the door. The air hung stale and sticky. She dialed the string of numbers that would get her into the United States, then Florida, then Miami. Because of the daily power failures and lack of phone lines, she could no longer use her laptop to e-mail, so this might be her only chance to reach home for a long time. The phone rang until she was almost ready to give up.

At last she heard a breathless "Hello."

"Amber? It's Heather."

"Oh my gosh! Is it really you? I can't believe it! How are you? Where are you?"

Emotion clogged Heather's throat. "I'm in Uganda. It's the middle of the day and I—I have so much to tell you, but not much time to talk." She explained her e-mail problem, then asked, "Are Mom and Dad there?"

"No, they're out," Amber said.

Heather felt the keen edge of disappointment. "Since I can't e-mail anymore, I'll have to start writing letters. Tell them—" Her voice cracked with emotion. "Tell them I love them and miss them."

"We miss you, too."

"I almost hung up. I thought you'd be out too."

"I'm grounded. Dylan and I stayed out past

curfew last weekend and Dad blew a gasket. Jeez, you'd think he could cut me a little slack now and then. I'm going stir-crazy around here." Amber paused. "Promise not to tell a secret?"

"My lips are zipped."

"I sneaked Dylan in. We're watching videos and swimming in the pool."

"You shouldn't—"

"Don't lecture me. Dad is such a pain these days. Let me tell you what happened yesterday. And it wasn't my fault either."

Heather held on to the receiver, listening but wanting to yell, *"Stop! Don't you know children are dying over here? Don't you know that there's something more important going on in the world than you being grounded?"* But she didn't interrupt.

"Mom and Dad hate me, Heather," Amber said, her voice suddenly low and sad. "I'd give anything if you'd come home. Can you? Can you just leave Africa early and come home right away?"

11

"Amber, I can't just pick up and leave. People are counting on me."

"But I need you," Amber wailed. "Things are impossible around here."

"How impossible?"

"Just yesterday, Dad took away my car keys."

"Why?"

"Because he's mean. And he hates me."

"Amber . . . ," Heather said in her best tell-me-the-rest-of-the-story voice.

"All right, so I'd gotten a parking ticket."

"And . . . ?"

"A speeding ticket too. But it wasn't my fault. Marsha was driving my car, and she got stopped for speeding, not me. But Dad says it's my responsibility because it's my car."

Heather sighed. Would her sister ever grow up? "Well, you can't make Dad change his mind once it's made up, so you'll just have to live with it."

"But school's started and I can't even drive to school! And he won't let Dylan take me either."

"School's already started?" Heather couldn't believe it. It seemed as if only yesterday she'd set out on the Mercy Ship. She had less than three months left in Africa.

"Hell-o," Amber said, drawing out the two syllables. "It's September. Don't you have a calendar over there?"

"Life's a bit different over here. . . . So, tell me, how are you getting to school?"

"The housekeeper's taking me. Can you imagine the humiliation of getting out of our housekeeper's car every day? I'm the joke of the senior class!"

"I can't change things for you, Amber. Even if I was stateside, I wouldn't be at home. I'd be in college and I couldn't come running home over every crisis." She heard Amber sigh.

"I know . . . but I can ask, can't I? Oh, before I forget, Joanie stopped by last week. She's on her way to college and wanted to make sure I told you she'd see you at Christmas."

"I appreciate the message. Listen, the line for the phone is growing, so I've got to go. But do yourself a favor and get Dylan out of there after we hang up. If Mom and Dad catch you, you'll be grounded until Christmas."

There was a moment of silence. "Okay," Amber said glumly. "But only because *you* asked me to. Before you hang up," she added in a rush, "are you all right? Are you having fun?"

There were a thousand things Heather wanted to say, but she was out of time. "Sure. Things are fine with me. Busy, but fine. I'm glad I came."

"How's Ian? You still revved about him?"

"Still revved," Heather said. "Tell Mom and Dad I'll write when I get to Lwereo. And take it easy on them, sis. They're old, you know."

Amber laughed. Once they'd hung up, homesickness swept over Heather. Her friends were going off to college, just as she would have been doing if she'd been home. But she wasn't home. She was where her dreams had taken her. She was in a world more different than even she had realized was possible. She loved her sister dearly, but Amber was a child—a petulant child who had no clue that two-thirds of the world did not have the luxury of a car. Or a home. Or food on the table every day.

Heather slipped from the phone booth, back into the world she'd come so far to see.

* * *

"Where are we going now?" Heather asked as she walked with Ian down a long, narrow sidewalk.

She had waited for him to finish his call home, and then he'd taken her by the hand and said, "Come with me."

Now he said, "We're going to the Delta. That's where all the cabs in Kampala wait for their fares."

"You mean the cabs don't come to the passengers?"

"How can they? Few phones, remember? The cabs wait in this one area and so you come to the Delta and find the cab that's headed out to where you want to go. When people want to come back into the city, they wait at special cab stops. The cab comes along eventually and picks them up. No buses here. Cabs and walking are the way people travel."

"They could ride their cows," Heather muttered under her breath.

The Delta was a half-block-wide dirt parking arena filled with minivans, the cabs of the city. Ugandans milled around, some hawking their services, others waiting patiently for their vans to fill so that they could be on their way. "No van moves until it's packed," Ian explained. "And each van holds fourteen to sixteen people."

Heather wondered how Amber would manage under such conditions, then decided she probably wouldn't. She hung close to Ian as he wove through the parked vans, asking a question or two in Swahili before moving on. Eventually he found the cab he was looking for, paid the driver, and ushered Heather inside. The space was cramped, but at least she had a window seat. Again she asked, "Where are we going?"

"To the Nalongo Orphanage. I want you to meet Mother Harriet."

The ride to the western outskirts of the city was bumpy and accompanied by clouds of dust. By the time they reached their destination, they were the only two left in the van. Ian asked the driver to wait, and the man parked under a nearby tree and turned off his engine. Immediately quiet descended.

"There it is," Ian said. They walked toward a midsized brick building with a tin roof sitting in a large field, shut off by a metal fence. He opened the gate.

"Can we do this?" she asked, half expecting guards to jump out.

"The gate means little. It's only a way to mark

the property," Ian told her. As they walked inside the fence, he added, "I met Mother Harriet when I was last here. She takes in street orphans, kids whose families have disappeared or been killed. I send her money to help out. Every little bit helps here."

They entered the building, and Heather stopped cold. The place was absolutely empty. She saw a dirt-smeared concrete floor and dirty, unpainted, peeling walls. Curtainless windows let in light, and a single bare bulb hung from a long cord in the center of the ceiling. She saw not one piece of furniture. "Have they moved?" she asked.

"No. This is the home of twenty-five children. This is their main activity room."

"B-But where do they live? Where do they sleep?"

"Their sleeping quarters are in the back. I'll show you, but first let's find Mother Harriet."

They found her in a small room off to one side, sitting behind a decrepit wooden desk piled with papers. She sprang up as they entered, a wide smile of recognition lighting her dark face. She was a tall woman, thin as a rail, and she wore a faded skirt and plaid top. Her hair was wrapped in a scarf.

"Mr. McCollum!" she cried. *"Habari."* She

greeted him in Swahili. "How good to see my fine Scottish benefactor. Why did you not tell me you were coming? I would have kept the children here, instead of sending them off to school."

"Mzuri," he answered, then said, "I did not know myself if there would be time to come by, so please excuse us dropping in unannounced." He introduced Heather.

"I will make us tea," Mother Harriet said. "Look around, then hurry back. Oh, and please see the fine dining table I was able to buy with some of the money you sent."

She hurried off into another room, and Ian took Heather by the elbow. "This way," he told her.

On the other side of the empty main room, they walked into a smaller room. There an old table stood, its top scratched and marred. It was quite long and fairly wide. "Where are the chairs?" Heather asked.

"I'm guessing that she couldn't afford chairs too."

"You mean the kids stand to eat?"

"Chairs are a luxury. It's better to buy food than a place to sit. And the table's used for many things besides eating. It was a good purchase."

"I—I can't believe they have so little." She thought of homeless shelters back home— she'd been in a few during her fund-raising efforts. Even though the kids who lived in the shelters were often destitute, they still had a recreation room with TV and toys.

"They have safety here. That's the best gift of all." Ian took her hand. "Come. There's more."

He led her down a corridor with a series of doorways. She stopped at the first one and saw six wooden beds covered with thin, colorful woven blankets. "A dormitory?" she asked.

"Yes. The kids are separated by age. The older ones stay here."

The walls were starkly bare, except for one window covered by aged striped curtains that fluttered in the faint breeze coming from outside. The window had no screen, so Heather knew there was no way to keep out mosquitoes—the main carriers of malaria and other diseases. Over one bed, someone had hung a tattered poster of Michael Jordan. Written on the walls surrounding the poster were threatening words about what would happen to anybody who touched it. On another bed, half stuffed beneath a thin pillow, she saw a ball of aluminum foil.

"They don't have much to call their own," Ian explained, following her glance. "So what they do have, they guard."

"But a *foil* ball?" Heather asked incredulously. "How can that be valuable to a kid?"

"It's all that's his," Ian said. "You have to understand that before coming here, they lived on the streets, begging or stealing food. Possessions, things a child can call his, are valuable indeed."

She wanted to slip something under every pillow, but she had brought nothing of value with her. No candy, very little money, and a bottle of water.

Next Ian took her outside, and Heather was glad to feel the warmth of the sun. The dormitory had depressed her and left her feeling cold.

"Over here is the garden," he said, walking her out to a large patch of cultivated land. She recognized rows of corn and cabbages. "They grow what food they can. Mother Harriet scrounges for the rest."

"How?"

"She begs local businesses. She writes letters to church groups in Europe and America. She's inventive and hard to refuse. But she's got a big job. It's not easy feeding twenty-five mouths two meals a day, three hundred and sixty-five days a year."

"She said they were in school. Where do they go to school?"

"They hold classes at a church in town with volunteers as teachers. They walk there and back every day. It's about ten kilometers—six miles."

"A long walk for a child," Heather said. She looked off into the distance and saw bedding—sheets and blankets—lying on the ground. "What's that?"

"It's an alternative to doing the laundry. Every few days, the children spread their sleeping things outside to catch the sun and kill the creepy crawlers in their pallets."

"Bugs? Ugh—don't they ever wash their clothes? How do they keep stuff clean?"

"They have no washing machines, you know. No running water, either. Water must be hand-carried up the hill from a pumping station almost a half mile away. When they do wash clothes, they boil water in pots and throw in the clothes with lye soap to get them clean. Then they hang them in the sun to dry." He grinned. "Our ancestors did the same thing. Unless, of course, they had servants to do the work."

She felt her cheeks flush as she realized that she had sounded judgmental. She must seem like a pampered princess to him. In truth, she could not dispute the impression. She did live a life of privilege. "You make me feel guilty."

"Heather, lass, you're curious. It's fine to ask questions. And you can't help where God saw fit to give you birth. He has blessed you, and it's nothing to feel shame for." His tone was kind, gentle. He pointed to a large metal tank on wooden stilts. "Recognize that?"

She'd seen one in Kenya. "It catches rainwater."

"Right. Good until the dry season comes, then it's down the hill for water."

A call from the building made them turn to Mother Harriet waving them inside. "Tea's ready!"

Back in her office, a wooden tray had been set with three cups and a china teapot. There was also a small plate holding three peeled, hardboiled eggs. "Eat. Our hens laid these just this morning," Mother Harriet said proudly.

Heather nibbled on her egg, feeling guilty, thinking that this was one less egg an orphan would get to eat. But she knew better than to refuse. Dr. Henry had told them in one of his sessions aboard the ship how insulting it was to refuse African hospitality. She sipped her tea from the chipped china cup and said, "Thank you. It's delicious."

The woman beamed at her. Then she turned to Ian and outlined her efforts to raise money. Heather listened, amazed—not by her efforts, but by the refusals she spoke of and the indifference to all Mother Harriet was trying to do to help children survive. Didn't the government care? Couldn't she get help from politicians? Heather wanted to ask a hundred questions but didn't. Ian was closing the conversation and standing. It was time to leave.

He reached inside his shirt and pulled out a wallet. "Take this," he said, and handed Mother Harriet a stack of folded money.

"Bless you," Mother Harriet said. "This will help us buy food. And I will be taking the youngest ones into the clinic for shots and medicine next week. The medicine is free, but they are too young to walk so far. Now I can take them by taxi."

She shook hands with Ian, and he and Heather walked to the van. The driver folded the newspaper he'd been reading and opened the door. Once they were on their way, Heather asked the questions she'd kept to herself before.

"The government is overloaded," Ian answered. "Almost half of the Ugandan population is under fifteen years old. The country is awash in orphans. Only a handful get taken into places like Mother Harriet's."

Heather's heart ached. She felt overwhelmed by what she'd seen that afternoon, impotent. She turned to Ian. "Why did you bring me here?"

He clasped his hand over hers and looked deep into her eyes. "We're going to Lwereo tomorrow, to the Kasana Children's Home. It's run by missionaries, with a thought for feeding both body and soul. They do things differently, and to my way of thinking, they do things better. I want you to judge for yourself, lass. I want you to see the children as I see them. Not through the eyes of men, but through the eyes of God."

12

The city of Lwereo was little more than a bump in the road. A few buildings, a town square, a soccer field—all clumped together within short walking distance of a village of thatched huts set back in the countryside. A turnoff onto a rutted dirt trail eventually brought the vans into a clearing. On one side was the Kasana mission hospital, on the other a gate with a sign: Children's Home.

Two young boys waved and opened the gate, and the vans drove through, stopping in an open area between several thatch-roofed buildings and a cinder-block ranch-style house. A young couple, surrounded by three blond boys, greeted Dr. Henry's group with hugs and smiles. The woman held a baby.

"I'm Paul Warring," the brown-haired man said. "And this is my wife, Jodene, and our sons,

Kevin, eight, Dennis, six, and Samuel, four. The baby"—Jodene waggled the baby's arm at the group—"is our eight-month-old daughter, Amie. Welcome."

Heather had not expected to see so young a couple here in the African bush. Paul was tall and trim, his wife petite and dainty, with shoulder-length blond hair and wire-rimmed glasses. The three boys kept jockeying for a position closest to their father's side, until Samuel fell and began to wail.

"Stop it, boys," Paul admonished. "We have guests. Who will show them to their rooms while I take Dr. Henry and Mr. Hoover inside for tea?"

The boys jumped up and down, begging for the job. Minutes later, Heather and the other girls were following Dennis into a dormitory-style building, where they found a living room furnished with a sofa and two chairs, and a small kitchen table and chairs. There were also two bedrooms, each with two beds.

"Wow!" exclaimed Ingrid. "This is wonderful! I thought we'd be pitching our tents again."

"Look," Cynthia announced with a grin, "indoor plumbing."

Heather was equally pleased. They had all

been expecting communal latrines like the ones they'd had in Kenya.

She went out for her bags and saw Ian sorting through the pile for his. "I didn't expect the place to be this nice," she told him.

"Yes, they've made some improvements since I was here last."

"And the Warrings . . . well, I thought they'd be old. And they're Americans, aren't they?"

Ian laughed. "They're from your North Dakota."

"Out west," she told him. "Wonder how they ended up in Uganda?"

"We're having a meeting in an hour. Why don't you ask them?" He tapped the end of her nose playfully. "See you there, lass."

The meeting was held under one of the thatched pavilions while the smell of grilling chicken wafted through the evening air. The kitchen was really a separate small hut set away from the other buildings but close to the house. The chickens cooked over open coals, watched carefully by a couple of Ugandan kids—residents of the home, Heather learned. Several enormous cast-iron pots filled with beans and corn sat atop a cement-and-brick stove, fueled by wood and charcoal.

"Before we eat," Paul began once everyone

had sat down on long wooden benches, "I want to thank each of you for coming so far, for giving up months of your real lives, to help out. I first came here on a mission trip when I was twenty-two, and returning to Uganda was a dream of mine for years.

"I'm a contractor by trade, and when I learned what my church organization planned to do over here, well, I begged Jodene to pull up stakes and come with me." He patted his wife's shoulder. "Thankfully, she agreed. That was three years ago. Jodene and I are the current overseers of the children's home, and we plan to remain here two more years.

"You see, Uganda is a country finally at peace after years of a military regime that killed over one million citizens before it was toppled. Thousands of people, mostly children, were left homeless and parentless. And it's these children we're hoping to help."

Heather listened with her heart. Here were people doing what she wanted to do. Here were people who were realizing their dream, in spite of the sacrifices they had to make. And by now, she understood what a sacrifice it was to leave family, friends, and country and come halfway around the world to help better the lives of strangers.

Paul continued. "We came here with a different philosophy. We base it on the old proverb. 'Give a man a fish and you feed him for a day. Teach a man to fish, and you feed him for a lifetime.' It wasn't enough to just take in orphans and care for them. We wanted to return the concept of fatherhood to these children's lives. First, we wanted them to see God as their heavenly father. To do that, they need an earthly father as a role model. Most of these kids don't even remember their parents or village life.

"Our goal is to train the oldest young men to become heads of families. The younger children are placed in these family groups, where they learn to live together much as they may have before they lost everything. With our supervision, the 'father' of these families is taught how to be responsible for his unit. Under his headship, his family learns to farm and raise livestock, which we supply; they learn a trade, such as carpentry or ornamental ironworking, sewing, or basket making—all the trades that their Ugandan forefathers learned and taught before the wars came. Eventually, the family members will grow up, move out, and create new villages. And, ultimately, marry and give birth and train up another generation.

"Everyone attends school daily here on the grounds, then spends time gardening or doing assigned chores. Our goal is to teach the youth skills and leave them self-sufficient and self-governing and able to fend for themselves once we return stateside.

"No one is forced to stay against his or her will. The door is always open for residents to leave. But if they stay, then they must obey the rules, which are mainly to work and go to school and live within one of our families."

Paul paused. "In the past three years, not one person has left." He looked over his audience. "Your being here is a blessing. Some of you will help build a new classroom. Some of you will begin teaching in our school. Others will work at the hospital on the other side of the road. None of you will be idle. You will never work harder, but you will never feel more useful.

"Now, if you want to ask questions, come to me during dinner. Right now, it's time to eat. That is, if you're hungry."

A deafening cheer went up. Heather stood, found Ian's gaze, and smiled. He winked, and she blew him a kiss.

Early the next morning, Heather showed up at the hospital along with Dr. Henry, Ian, and her roommate Cynthia. The hospital grounds were neat and well kept, the flower beds ablaze with pink and red blossoms. Patients who were ambulatory sat outside under banana trees in old-fashioned wooden wheelchairs and on benches positioned along the porch. They played cards, read newspapers, or talked with family and friends. Heather saw none of the high-tech equipment she was used to in American hospitals. IV stands held glass bottles rather than soft plastic bags, and rubber rather than plastic tubing. Traction for a man with multiple broken bones was a system of ropes and wooden pulleys instead of stainless steel and slim cables.

Inside, the hospital smelled of antiseptic and soap. The walls were painted yellow; the floors were bare concrete, still damp and shiny after being mopped. Banks of windows allowed morning sunlight to flood the wards, where white metal beds lined the walls. The beds reminded Heather of ones she'd seen in old war movies.

She learned that she and Cynthia would work with the nurses, while Dr. Henry and Ian would see patients and help in the operating room. The doctor in charge, Dr. Gallagher, was Irish, and he and his family lived in a small house on hospital property. The other two doctors were Ugandan—second-year residents on loan from hospitals in England, where they were getting their medical training. There were also six full-time nurses, three of them nuns, all of them Ugandans. Dr. Gallagher's wife was also a nurse, but she worked only when there was a crisis.

Dr. Gallagher walked them through the facility, showing them the women's and men's wards—two wings of the building, connected by a central receiving area. Rooms off the central area contained the lab, the clinic, a small lounge where cots were set up for night personnel, and a room for sick infants. The babies were kept not in plastic Isolettes, but in hand-carved wooden cradles. There was no neonatal intensive care unit.

"The operating and recovery room is off the men's ward," Dr. Gallagher explained in his heavy Irish accent. "The building out back is the isolation wing. That's where we keep the tuberculosis patients, the contagious cases that come in, and AIDS victims in the final stages of their disease."

His words sent a chill through Heather. In America, AIDS victims had an arsenal of drugs that often kept their disease at bay; here there was no such hope. The treatments were simply too costly. Dr. Gallagher explained that the best they could do was to keep the patient as comfortable as possible until he or she died.

Heather recalled what Patrick had told her on the ship—multiple wives, multiple sex partners had spread the disease quickly through the population. And when Dr. Gallagher explained that part of their work as aides would include counseling women in the clinic on family planning and HIV awareness, Heather realized that her job was going to be more than cleaning bedpans and keeping track of paperwork.

She and Cynthia went straight to work with Sister Della, tackling a maze of jobs that included changing patients' bandages and dispensing medications. The morning passed so quickly that Heather was shocked when Ian stuck his head in the door and reminded her that it was time for a lunch break. "I don't know if I can take a break," she told him.

"You must. We can't have you dropping over the first day on the job."

He took her outside to a bench beneath a graceful old tree and spread a white napkin between them. He opened a small canvas bag and took out two bottles of water, a few bananas, a pile of cooked rice wrapped in a banana leaf, two boiled eggs, and a baked sweet potato.

Heather hadn't realized how hungry she was until she smelled the food. "Tastes good," she said, eating a sweet, finger-sized banana in one bite. "Where'd you get it?"

"Jodene sent it over. She knew none of us had thought about lunch. I gave a bag to Cynthia and Dr. Henry, too."

"I guess there's no cafeteria or vending machines around here," Heather said. "When I worked in the hospital back home, food was never a problem."

"They prepare food in a cookhouse out back for the patients. For some, it's the only time they eat regular." He took a bite of sweet potato. "How was your morning?"

"Busy. How about yours?"

"Stitched up a man who'd fallen in a ditch, and assisted Dr. Henry in the OR, setting a broken leg. Greenstick fracture—bone came clear through the skin."

She grimaced.

She saw that a bandage had been taped to the inside of Ian's elbow and asked about it.

"Gave blood. I'm O negative, the universal

donor. The man needed a transfusion, and the lab had no blood, so I rolled up my sleeve."

"You gave blood right there in the OR?" She couldn't imagine her parents stopping an operation to give blood to one of their patients, although she knew that her father donated blood on occasion to the hospital's blood bank.

"A person does what he has to," Ian said matter-of-factly.

The news unsettled her, making her wonder if the man would have died if Ian hadn't been there. "I guess I could give blood too," she said.

"If you can spare a pint, the lab can use it. Dr. Gallagher said some should be coming next week, but in the meantime, we may have an emergency. All the doctors and nurses give blood regularly. It's part of the job."

"I have some syringes my dad made me bring."

"Smart thinking," Ian said. "Dr. Gallagher runs a good hospital. He never reuses needles."

She was glad of that—she didn't want Ian running any unnecessary risks.

"Lass, I believe lunch is over," he said looking past her shoulder. "Here comes an ambulance."

Surprised because she hadn't heard a siren, Heather turned. She saw no vehicle, just four men carrying a litter attached to long poles that rested on their shoulders. A woman covered by a blanket lay on the stretcher. A man and a small child tagged along behind. "*That's* the ambulance?"

Ian stood, scooping up the debris from their lunch. "Yes. They probably walked all night from the bush to bring her. I'd better go see to her problem."

She watched him trot toward the stretcher bearers, move alongside, and take the woman's wrist, feeling for a pulse.

Something bad had happened to the woman, of that Heather was certain. But there had been no 911 emergency service to call for help. For her there had only been the men of her village to carry her to the nearest hospital. For her there had been hours, maybe days of pain. And maybe, like the baby Heather had held in Kenya, the woman was already beyond help.

A chill ran through Heather as she watched the men walk into the hospital, followed closely by the other man and the child, who began to cry for his mother.

13

Heather's days quickly fell into a routine. Six days a week, she worked at the hospital. On Sunday, she joined everyone in the compound for church services, where Miguel's guitar music was added to the African flute and drums. Sunday afternoon was free time, and Sunday evening, the entire camp came together for dinner and prayer.

She loved her work. She and Cynthia shared stories from the hospital with Ingrid and Debbie, who had their own stories about teaching in the school. "The children are bright," Ingrid often said. "And so eager to learn. At the end of the day, I feel like a dried-out sponge."

Under Bob Hoover's direction, the construction project took shape, and by the middle of October, a concrete slab had been poured and cinder blocks had risen to form walls.

Boyce, Miguel—all the kids working on the building had turned nut brown under the African sun, and their bodies bulged with well-toned muscles.

Ian spent long hours in the OR or sitting by the bedsides of critical patients, adjusting IVs and doling out pain medications, always in short supply. Once every two weeks, a Red Cross truck arrived with supplies, but the hospital never knew if it would be the supplies they desperately needed or an overabundance of something they didn't. Every day was an adventure.

One Saturday evening, Paul and Jodene invited Dr. Henry, Bob, and Ian to the house for dinner. Ian asked Heather to join them, and she found herself frantically sorting through her duffel bags for something pretty to wear.

"Wear my silver hoops," Ingrid offered, dangling the pretty earrings under Heather's nose.

"How about my long skirt?" Cynthia said, shaking out a lovely aqua skirt with lace insets.

"I have one unstained white blouse," Debbie said. "It's yours for the night."

"I love you all," Heather said, tying up her hair with a white ribbon and dabbing a few drops of perfume behind her ears.

Just before she was to leave, Ingrid pulled

her to one side. "You are very pretty. Ian will be moved."

Heather blushed. Was it that obvious that she was dressing for him and not for dinner? She'd told no one except Amber, thousands of miles away, how she felt about Ian, and even then she hadn't expressed the depth of her feelings. "He's been nice to me," Heather said to Ingrid. "But I know I shouldn't read too much into it."

Ingrid shrugged. "He is a fine person, and yes, handsome too. It is not hard to see why you care for him."

"It's not a dumb crush. It—It's different."

"*Ja*," Ingrid said with a matter-of-fact nod. "This I can see by the look on your face."

"Oh, great," Heather moaned. "Don't tell me that."

"But it is true. And tonight you are beautiful for him." Ingrid smiled and patted Heather's arm. "He will be—how do you say it?—bowled over."

When Ian arrived to fetch Heather, the look on his face told her that Ingrid had made a good call.

Jodene served dinner at a long, narrow table that had been hewn from a single log. The underside was still rough and curved, the top sanded smooth. Kerosene lamps and candles lit the room. "We have a gas generator," Paul explained, "but we try and make do without it because gasoline is so expensive."

Heather didn't mind. She found the atmosphere charming.

Jodene served an egg "pizza," the crust formed from crackers. There was a bowl of pilau—rice mixed with spices—and the ever-plentiful *matoke*, which Heather had never developed a taste for. But she found the conversation wonderful, surprised at how hungry her ears were for sounds of English words pronounced with American accents.

She was helping herself to a dessert of pineapple and mango when she caught a movement out of the corner of her eye. On the other side of the room, peeking from under a cot beside the sofa, she saw the dark face of a child. Startled, Heather set down her fork and turned for a better look. "Who's that?" she asked.

Jodene gently pushed back her chair and crossed to the cot, knelt down, and held out her hand. "Kia, would you like to come out and meet our friends?"

The child crawled farther under the cot.

"They won't hurt you, Kia." The child refused to budge, and Jodene returned to the table. "Sorry, she's not coming out."

"Who is she?" Heather asked.

"It's a sad story," Paul said, hunching over the table. "She came here about three months ago with her mother. They were Sudanese and somehow had made it out of a refugee camp into Uganda. Problem was, Kia's mother was desperately sick. She died within a couple of weeks, and we took in Kia."

"Poor little girl! How old is she?"

"We're guessing four or five. Poor nutrition has left her small for her age, but Dr. Gallagher checked her over and that was his guess. The boys have tried to befriend her, but she won't have anything to do with them. She's fascinated with Amie, however."

At this point, Jodene took up the story. "Her mother had a photograph with her. Here." She fished in a desk drawer and pulled out a Polaroid snapshot of little Kia and a woman holding a baby—a baby whose face was tragically deformed.

"Cleft palate," Dr. Henry said studying the picture. "We can correct that with surgery. Where's the infant now?"

"A health worker took the photo. It helps

keep relatives together when they come into the camp. According to the mother's story, a worker took the baby to the infirmary. Somehow, she was able to get herself and Kia out of the country, but in the turmoil, she had to leave the baby. By the time she arrived here, she was sick and delirious. Still, she kept pleading with us to go get her daughter in Sudan."

"Can't you go to the camp and get the baby?"

Paul shook his head. "Not legally. You can't just walk in and take a child, and going through the proper channels is almost impossible. Red tape five miles long. Why, she'd be half grown if we went that route."

"What are you going to do?" asked Heather. "She needs surgery. I mean, my parents fix that kind of defect all the time."

Dr. Henry spoke up. "We can certainly repair her face back on the ship."

But Heather knew that the ship had sailed on by now and wouldn't return for another year. It was too long for the baby to wait. "Are you saying the baby's case is hopeless?" she asked.

"Not totally," Paul answered. "We have a friend, Dr. Ed Wilson. He's just come over as a volunteer to do medical service in the Sudanese camps. He's on the lookout for the baby."

"This kind of deformity makes it difficult for babies to suckle," Dr. Henry said. "And it's hard to say if someone is even going to the trouble of feeding her in the camps. Did the mother say anything about any other family members?"

Paul shook his head. "We surmise that hers was one of hundreds of small villages destroyed by the rebels. What's happening over there is pretty brutal stuff and not dinner conversation, but thousands have fled and are packed into these camps. Relief and health workers are overwhelmed by the sheer numbers of displaced survivors."

"How will you know if he finds her?" Ian asked.

"Ham radio," Paul said. "It's the only way we have to communicate around here. Our families in the U.S. have ham radios, and that's how we keep in touch. Ed is supposed to notify us if he turns up anything." Paul cut his eyes toward Kia, still crouched under the cot. "If she's still alive," he added in a lowered voice.

Heather felt such pity for Kia that tears welled in her eyes. "Doesn't she ever come out from under the cot?"

Jodene shook her head. "Hardly ever. She

runs outside to go to the bathroom. She eats when I put food beside the cot. She won't sleep on top of the cot, either. She sleeps under it, like a frightened animal. We tried to put her into one of the family units, but she ran away and came straight back here. Maybe because it was the place she last saw her mother alive."

Jodene chewed on her lip reflectively. "We'll never know what really happened to Kia and her family, but whatever happened totally traumatized her. And in all the time she's been here, she's never spoken a word. I know she understand us. Sometimes she sits and rocks and wails, so we know she can make sound, but she never speaks. Not one single word since her mother died. The only other person she has in the world is her baby sister. I would give *anything* if we could reunite them."

Once dinner was over, Ian and Heather went for a walk on the grounds, where the fronds of banana trees rustled, lending a kind of music to the night. Under the star-studded sky, the full moon floated above them like a ghost ship, adrift on an inky sea, and lit the landscape with a pale light.

"Thanks for inviting me tonight," she told

Ian. "Except for hearing about Kia, the evening was perfect."

"Yes, lass. It's a sad story. And there are so many sad stories. But the girl's with good people. Jodene and Paul will help her however they can. You know, I believe one by one a difference is made."

Heather held out her hand as if to catch the moonbeams. "If I could," she said, "I'd bring Kia these moonbeams. Maybe they would make her smile glow."

"Just the way yours glows," Ian said, looking at her and making her heart skip.

"It's only the moonlight."

"No, lass. It's *your* glow. It begins down deep in your heart and bubbles up till it spills out your eyes."

"If you want me to melt at your feet, keep it up."

He laughed, the sound rich and deep. "You make my days brighter, Heather. You make this place a better place for your being here. Sometimes, when I'm sitting with a patient I know will not live through the night, I think of you. I hold on to the patient, but my mind is all around you. It helps me let go of what I cannot change."

"It's the same for me, Ian." Her words came

out breathlessly. She found it difficult to give voice to the things she'd held silently in her heart for so long. "I can't picture my life without you in it."

"Careful. . . . I will not let you take back these words."

"I don't want to take them back. I can't help the way I feel."

"Feelings grow stronger in the moonlight. It's strange but true."

"I feel the same way in the clear light of day. I—I want to be with you."

He toyed with her hoop earring, saying nothing for such a long time that she was afraid she'd said far too much. She knew she was younger than he. She knew that he had plans and dreams that had never included her. But she also knew how she felt. She loved him. Although he'd never kissed her, never romanced her, never so much as hinted that she was anything more to him than a pretty girl on a mission trip, he had taken root inside her heart in such a way that she wasn't sure she could ever uproot him.

"This trip will end," he said finally. "You'll go back to your home; I'll return to mine. I have years to go before I finish my schooling. And you have college, too. You told me so. You'll want to go on with your life when you get home."

Her other life didn't seem important now. Here in the moonlight, under the stars of Africa, she wasn't sure she had another life. But *he* did. Was he telling her he had no room in it for her? "It's hard to think about that now," she said with a nervous laugh. "Must be moon madness."

"Yes," he whispered. "That's possible."

More than anything, she wanted to throw herself into his arms, have him smother her with kisses. More than anything, she wanted to say, "I love you," and hear him tell her the same. But he knew what he wanted for his future. She knew she shouldn't muddy his waters, cloud his dreams. It wouldn't be fair.

She stepped away and said in a forced, bright voice, "I promised Dr. Gallagher I'd come in early tomorrow, and if I don't get some sleep . . . well, I'll be dragging all day."

"I know. Me too."

They fell into step together beneath the moon and walked quickly back to the guest dormitory, touching shoulders but not speaking.

14

"I can't stop thinking about Kia." Heather was sitting on a bench with Ian outside the hospital.

"I know what you mean, lass. I think of her often myself."

It was a rare afternoon when they had both finished their day's work a bit early. Heather thought he looked exhausted, but she'd been wanting to talk to him about Kia for days. "I talked to Jodene with some ideas about getting Kia to open up," she said. "Back home, when I worked at the hospital as a volunteer for a summer, I helped with some autistic children."

"I don't think Kia is autistic."

"I agree. But I asked Jodene if I could try some of the things that worked with those kids."

Ian shut his Bible, which had been lying

open on his lap. Sun dappled his hair through the trees. "What things?"

"Well, every afternoon this past week, I've visited Jodene's and sat myself down on the floor next to the cot. I just sit there and hum to myself, paying no special attention to Kia, who stays hidden. I stay for about thirty minutes, and when I go, I leave a piece of candy. Jodene says Kia's been eating it."

"Yes, but she eats all food placed by the cot."

"I know, but I worked late on Friday, so I was late getting to the house. Jodene says Kia crawled out from under the cot and went to the window and looked out. She thinks Kia might have been looking for me."

"That's a good conclusion."

Encouraged by Ian's approval, Heather added, "I want her to trust me. She needs to trust someone again. She needs to come back into the real world."

"You're right, lass. She can't spend the rest of her life hiding under a cot."

"I feel so sorry for her. But I don't know if I'm the person to help her. I mean, I'll be leaving in another few weeks, and I can't take her with me. Maybe I should leave the job to someone more qualified."

Ian tilted his head, appraising her with his

intelligent blue eyes. "Have you ever read the Book of Esther?"

"Not for a long, long time. But what's that got to do with Kia?"

He opened his Bible, which was stuffed with notes on bits of paper. "It tells of how the Jewish people came to celebrate the festival of Purim, a celebration of their deliverance from annihilation at the hands of the Persians.

"At the time, the Jews were captives of King Xerxes, but they'd been living in Persia for so long that they had their own cities, homes, businesses, and normal, everyday lives. Anyway, the current queen fell from the king's favor, so he had all the young women of his kingdom brought in so that he could choose a new queen. He chose Esther, without ever knowing she was a Jew.

"The king had a wicked advisor, Haman, who hated the Jews, especially Mordecai, who, unknown to him, happened to be Esther's uncle. Haman plotted how he could destroy every Jew in his country, devised a plan, and even got the king to agree to it. So Mordecai sent Esther a message, asking her to plead with the king for mercy and spare their people." Ian opened his Bible and read, " 'For if you remain silent at this time, relief and deliverance for the Jews will arise from another place.' " Ian glanced up. "You see, Mordecai believed God *would* deliver them, one way or another, but he believed Esther was their best hope.

"Mordecai asked her, 'And who knows but that you have come to royal position for such a time as this?' " Ian turned to Heather. "But in those days, no one—not even the queen—could come into the king's presence unless the king summoned her. Queen Esther would be risking her life to go before the king without being invited. It would take phenomenal courage for her to leave her life of comfort and security in the king's court and face possible death.

"So Esther asked all her people to fast and pray for her, saying, 'When this is done, I will go to the king, even though it is against the law. And if I perish, I perish.' " Ian closed his Bible. "You know the rest of the story, don't you, lass?"

Heather, caught up in his telling of it, nodded but didn't speak.

Ian said, "Esther went to the king, and he received her. He heard her petition and granted it. In the end, Haman was hanged on the gallows he'd constructed for Mordecai, and Mordecai, the Jew, rose to a position of power and honor. Because of Esther's courage."

"Why are you telling me this, Ian?"

"Because we must always look at life in the grand scheme of God's sovereignty. Perhaps you have come to Uganda 'for such a time as this.' To help bring Kia back into life."

Tears misted Heather's eyes. "Maybe to balance out the baby I couldn't save," she whispered. "Maybe this one and not that one."

Ian's hand closed over hers. "God's given you a heart for caring, lass. I learned that almost from the first time we met. It's a wondrous gift, and I can't think of anyone I'd like to see use it more than you."

Their fingers intertwined, his flesh warm and firm in hers, and the moment seared itself into Heather's heart—the sunlight on the grass, the shadows flickering through the leaves, the soft breath of a lemon-scented breeze. All came together. She knew it would be a memory as vivid as any photograph. And one that she would hold in her heart forever.

For the next three weeks, Heather went to Jodene's every day after work, sat on the floor in front of the cot, and pretended to be interested in everything except Kia. She played board games with the three boys, bounced balls, played jacks and Pickup Sticks by herself. She sang and talked, and she laid a piece of wrapped hard candy under the cot when she left. Kia never ventured out.

"I'm running low on candy," Heather confided to Jodene one Sunday evening after the group dinner. "And I don't think I'm making any progress."

"I think you are. Kia crawled out yesterday and watched us eat dinner. She's never done that before."

Heather felt a spark of encouragement. "Did she do anything else?"

Jodene thought a moment. "She still peeks out the window if you're running late. And while she always goes outside to go to the bathroom, she's staying outdoors longer. She sits and plays with the dirt, lets it run through her fingers, like she's reconnecting with it somehow."

"That sounds good." Heather thought for a moment. "Listen, I have an idea. Tomorrow, instead of coming inside, I'm going to sit under the tree in your front yard. If she looks out the window, she'll see me. Maybe she'll come outside to be with me."

"It's worth a try."

Over the weeks, Heather had grown to admire and respect Jodene. She cooked her family's meals on a hot plate, or on open coals in the cooking hut outside her kitchen door. She washed dishes with rainwater under a hand pump mounted on her kitchen sink—which was a wooden counter with a large plastic bowl. She washed clothes, including Amie's diapers, by hand with the help of some of the older girls living on the premises. There was an endless line of laundry hanging out to dry.

"You need a washing machine," Heather told her.

"How would I plug it in?" Jodene answered with a grin. "Believe me, gas for the generator costs more than the energy to do it by hand."

Kevin and Dennis went to school with the Ugandan children, and after school they all played together, as carefree as colts romping in spring meadows. Heather compared them with herself as she was growing up. She'd had plenty to do—Montessori school, dance lessons, even two years of gymnastics for her and Amber—but she never recalled the sheer joy she saw reflected in the boys' faces.

In November, Jodene told all the Americans

in the compound to prepare to come to the house for Thanksgiving dinner. "It's when I miss home most of all," she told Heather. "I come from a big family, and every year we'd gather at my parents' home and have a feast fit for a Roman orgy."

Heather had all but forgotten Thanksgiving was approaching. At her house, the holiday meant going away on ski trips out West. She hadn't had a turkey dinner at home in six years. "I'll spread the word," she told Jodene. "But won't the others feel left out?"

"Thanksgiving is uniquely American, so no one cares about it but us. My mother sent me a care package with the missionary group that stopped by in October. So I have goodies to share."

Heather had learned that the missionary circle was small but well connected. No missionaries came through without goods from the States for those serving in Uganda. Whenever possible, reliable travelers hand-carried mail stateside for the missionary community. Nobody mailed packages in or out of the country because they never made it out of the airport, where local police, guards, and other officials helped themselves to whatever they wanted.

As for Heather, she had written several letters home, but mail pickup and delivery were sporadic. So she didn't hear from home often, and when she did, the news was weeks old. The last word she'd received had been all about October's homecoming and how Amber had been chosen for the court.

"I have something to bring for the feast too," Heather told Jodene.

"What?" Jodene's eyes lit up.

"I'll surprise you. In fact, I'll tell everybody to bring something to share."

No one was more ecstatic about the upcoming dinner than Boyce. "Hot dog," he drawled, "count me in. I'll find something to bring besides an appetite."

Thanksgiving. Now that she was so far from home, how special it seemed to Heather. She didn't care if they ate *matoke*, she just wanted to be with everybody for the holiday. It didn't even bother her that Ian would not be there. After all, he was Scottish, and the celebration meant nothing to him. "I'll work," he said. "You have your special day, lass, and enjoy it. Tell me all about it later."

Four days before the holiday, Heather went to Jodene's to help make table decorations: cutout paper turkeys, pilgrim hats, and cornucopias. They were working at the kitchen table by lamplight when Paul came out of his and Jodene's bedroom, looking excited.

"I've been on the ham radio," he said in a low voice as he leaned over the table. "I talked with Ed Wilson. He's located Kia's sister."

15

Heather's heart thudded expectantly. "He found her? How is she?"

Paul glanced toward the cot. "I'd rather not talk in here. Let's go outside, and Heather, can you find Ian and bring him to hear this? He wanted to know when the baby was found."

She wasted no time in locating Ian, who was having a Bible study with some of the older Ugandan teens living in the compound. By the time the two of them had returned to Paul and Jodene's, Paul had dragged four chairs into the front yard, and Jodene had put some candles on the windowsill. The flames flickered and danced, casting a pale yellow light into the circle of chairs.

"Heather says Kia's sister's been found," Ian said as he settled into a chair.

"It's true. I heard from Ed tonight."

"How is she?"

"Not good."

Heather's stomach tightened with the news.

Paul continued. "She's in the clinic at the camp, but conditions there are pretty grim. If not for the kindness of a nun, who's been feeding her with a special syringe several times a day, the baby would be dead already."

Heather recalled Dr. Henry's saying that babies with cleft palates didn't suckle well, so Kia's sister probably couldn't take a bottle. Heather realized that hand-feeding her had to be painstaking work, and she silently blessed the nun for taking on this labor of love.

"What about IV feeding?" Ian asked.

"Ed's got her on a drip now, but equipment and supplies are in high demand, and frankly, they're needed for more critical patients. He says the situation at the camp is chaotic. People line up under a tree for immunizations, and a few cases of cholera have broken out. Some nights they can hear rebel gunfire in the distance." Paul stopped talking, as if to let the bleakness of the situation sink in.

"Is there anything we can do to help?" Jodene asked. "It sounds as if, if we don't do something, she'll die."

Heather saw Paul and Ian exchange glances.

"We've been discussing it beforehand," Ian said. "Ever since I learned about Kia's sister."

Heather sat up straighter.

"I know that I have much to do here," Ian said, "but we all know that choosing to help this one is a special thing for all of us. So I'm going to fetch her. My mind's made up."

No one said anything.

"Isn't there anyone else who can go?" Heather finally ventured.

"I'm the best candidate. I have medical skills she'll need."

Paul nodded. "I agree."

"How will you get there?"

Paul said, "There's an air service—Mission Air—in Kampala that flies old DC-3s left over from World War Two into Sudan and Rwanda. They fly in most of our workers for the refugee camps, as well as World Health professionals and volunteers."

Heather knew that commercial airlines flew only into Entebbe; this was the first she'd heard of any other air service in the country. But World War II planes? They were ancient!

"The planes are old and without any refinements, but the pilots keep them in good mechanical condition," Paul explained, as if he'd read her mind. "Plus, they usually don't get any flak from authorities for doing humanitarian service. Of course, if there's shooting going on and a person absolutely must get in or out of either country, well, he can hire mercenary pilots. They fly small Cessnas under the radar. It's risky and expensive, but it's a way to get in and out."

Heather felt the blood leave her face. *Shooting? Mercenaries? Evading radar?* She didn't want Ian facing those kinds of dangers for any reason!

They talked some more, laying plans, but Heather could hardly bear to listen. And when Ian walked her back to her room, she told him how she felt.

"Please, don't concern yourself for me. Think about the look on Kia's face when she sees her sister. That's the prize for going."

They were almost to the room when they ran into Dr. Henry and Patrick coming from the village. Ian quickly filled them in on what was happening. It maddened Heather that neither of them spoke a single word of discouragement.

"I'll drive you into Kampala myself," Dr. Henry said. "When do you want to leave?"

"Paul says the planes only fly once a week, on Tuesday around noon."

"We'll leave on Monday, stay at the guest house."

"Why can't Patrick go?" Heather blurted out her question. "He's Ugandan and he's studying medicine. Why can't he go?"

The three men regarded her, but it was Patrick who spoke up. "I am Hutu, not Tutsi," he said, as if that explained everything. "Kia and her sister are Tutsi. The officials would not let a Hutu take a Tutsi child from the camp. Ian is white. And a doctor—or almost. People will look the other way."

"What are you talking about? What's a Hutu?"

"It is my tribe. In Africa, a person's tribe is most important, and the Hutu is one of the largest tribes. Most Ugandans are Hutu. The fighting in Sudan and Rwanda is due to militant Hutu rebels killing Tutsi."

Heather just stared at the three men. "They *kill* each other just because they're from different tribes? Why doesn't someone stop them?"

"No one can stop them," Patrick said.

"It's genocide. Ethnic cleansing," Dr. Henry added.

"But why do they do it?"

"It's about power," Patrick said. "Control of

the land. The Hutu rebels have killed thousands. Sudanese villagers have fled, looking for safety. Some get into neighboring countries. Most flee to the refuge camps, hoping to return to their villages . . . what's left of them. The world governments cannot police every country. They can protest and step in to help the victims, but Africa belongs to the Africans, the different tribes, and they must work things out among themselves."

Heather didn't know what to say. She had heard about the fighting in Africa, but she hadn't realized how much of it stemmed from tribal roots. "But you're different, Patrick. You're not that way. You're not going to kill anyone."

He gave her a kindly smile. "I am a Christian, Heather. When I became one, in my heart, I put away my tribal history and differences. But I cannot put away who I am to the Tutsi. They hate me on sight. In your War Between the States, brothers killed brothers. Our two countries are not so different."

She looked from one face to the other, seeing the big picture in ugly clarity. People in Africa were dying, murdered by their own. Kia's entire village had been destroyed simply because she belonged to the wrong tribe. Heather felt foolish—incredibly stupid. She had wanted to come to Africa to save starving children. Save them for what?

"It's getting late," Ian said.

Dr. Henry shook Ian's hand. "We'll talk more tomorrow."

Patrick bade them good evening and left.

When they were alone, Ian took her hands in his. "I will bring the baby here, lass. Don't be afraid for us."

She nodded, fighting tears. "You must go get her, Ian. Without you, she has no other hope."

Once word got around that Ian was heading off to rescue Kia's sister, friends came to wish him well. Boyce told him, "If you want company, I'll come along."

"I'll need to travel light," Ian said. "But thanks for the offer. And I'll need you to stay and keep a watch over everyone." He looked straight at Heather as he said it, and it made her heart beat faster.

On the Sunday before Thanksgiving, during church, prayers were said for Ian to have a successful mission. There was always a possibility that something would go wrong and he wouldn't be able to get the baby out of Sudan.

Her health was fragile, and that was also worrisome. What if she was too ill to travel?

Once evening had fallen and Heather found herself finally alone with Ian, she was hesitant to say good night.

Ian told her, "The plan is to fly in Tuesday and back to Kampala on Wednesday. Dr. Henry will stay in Kampala, pick us up as soon as we land, and we'll come here on Thursday. We'll be home before you finish with that holiday dinner Jodene has planned."

"You think so?" Having him back on Thursday would be the best Thanksgiving blessing of all.

"Yes." He smiled at her, his face bathed in moonlight. "And while I'm gone, you keep working with Kia. Her sister will need her eventually . . . once her palate is repaired. They can live here with one of the overseers and be a family again."

The image of Kia and her sister staying at the children's home, growing up safe and happy within a new family unit, made Heather feel better. They deserved the chance. "All right, I'll keep trying to reach Kia. And I'll count the minutes until you return."

Ian was gazing down at her, and she couldn't

control the beating of her heart. She rose on tiptoe and kissed his cheek. He caught her elbows and pulled her closer. "You know, lass," he said, his voice but a whisper in the night, "I would not forgive myself if I went so far away and didn't do what I have wanted to do since I met you."

"And what would that be?" Her words trembled with emotion.

"I would like to kiss you, lass. If I have your permission, that is."

"Not only my permission," she said, "but my blessing."

He held her face between the palms of his hands and lowered his mouth to hers. His lips were soft, his kiss breathtaking. Heather felt her knees go weak while pinpricks of light spun behind her closed eyes. She poured her soul into the kiss, hoping to tell him how much she loved him, how much he meant to her.

He pulled away, his breath ragged, and wrapped his arms around her. He held her against his chest, and she felt the thumping of his heart. She buried her face in his shirt, clinging to him like a flower needing rain. He smoothed her hair, kissed the top of her head. "I love you, Heather. I didn't want to speak of it, but I can't help myself. I love you, and when

I come back, we must speak of it together." He lifted her chin, and she saw that his expression was worried. "You don't mind that I kissed you?"

She smiled then, unable to contain her joy. "One question: What took you so long to get around to it?"

16

On Monday afternoon, Heather went straight from the hospital to Jodene's, where she sat down under a tree in clear view of the house. She placed a ring of candy in plain sight and opened a book. Time passed. From the corner of her eye, she saw Kia looking at her through the window. Heather waited expectantly, but Kia never came outside. When Heather finally gave up, she left a piece of candy on the ground for the child.

On Tuesday, the same thing happened. On Wednesday, she heard a movement in the bushes and looked to see Kia peeking at her from the foliage. Heather made eye contact, smiled and beckoned to the child to come. "I have candy," Heather said, holding open her hand. Kia lowered her gaze, then ran back inside the house.

Disappointed, Heather returned to her room, where Ingrid was grading papers.

"No luck?" Ingrid asked.

"She was off like a scared rabbit," Heather said, flopping onto the sofa. "I'm not reaching this child."

"Do not blame yourself. You have worked hard and tried your best."

"But time's running out. We're leaving in two weeks." She looked at the calendar Debbie had hung on the wall. The days were marked off in red, with the second Thursday in December circled and labeled *D-Day*. That was the day the minivans would come to pick them up for the drive to Entebbe airport. There they would board the British Airways plane that would take them to London, and from London they would each go their separate ways. At least Heather would be traveling on with the other Americans into Miami's airport—her final destination. All in all, the trip took two long, hard days.

Heather fluffed a pillow and stretched out. "Maybe when Kia sees her sister she'll begin to trust us. I keep telling myself how hard it must be for her. Ripped from her home and her family and plopped down with a bunch of strangers. And white strangers to boot."

Ingrid smiled. "*Ja,* we are a scary bunch."

Heather laughed. "I'll miss you, Ingrid."

"Same here."

"Will you come again?"

"I am not sure. My parents want me to finish at the university. I need to get my teaching license; then I can come as a real teacher. How about you?"

"I want to come back, and I don't want to wait until next summer."

"Could it be because of Ian?"

Heather sighed. "He's returning to school in Scotland."

"But you will write each other, *ja?*"

"I'll sure write to *him.* We've been together every day for almost six months. I can't imagine getting up every day and not seeing him."

"I will write to Boyce too. I have grown accustomed to him and the funny things he says. I will miss him, too."

Heather sat up, hugging the pillow to herself. "I didn't come over here to fall in love. It just sort of happened."

Ingrid nodded and grinned. "*Ja.* Love is like that—it just happens. I wish you and Ian much luck and happiness."

Heather knew she would need it. Miami was

an ocean away from Scotland and a lifetime away from Africa.

On Thanksgiving Day, six Americans showed up at the Warrings'—all except for Dr. Henry, who had remained in Kampala to await Ian's return. Paul said, "Before we eat, we're going into Lwereo to watch a soccer game. I mean, what's Thanksgiving without football?"

When they arrived, the stands were already packed with local fans, people who'd walked for miles through the surrounding countryside to get to the game. Heather and her friends squeezed into the pack and quickly chose their favorites.

"I've got to go with the guys in red and white," Boyce said. "Alabama's colors."

"Good choice," Paul said. "That's the local team, and if you cheered for the other side, you could cause a riot."

The playing field was rough and uneven, the goals' nets had large holes in them, and the players spanned a wide age range, but the crowd treated the team as though it were composed of superstars playing in the World Cup. Heather tried to get interested, but her thoughts kept returning to Ian. She was seated beside Jodene, and during the half, she asked, "Has it been hard to raise your kids so far from home? I see how hard you work."

Jodene pushed back her blond hair and smiled. "I came from a family of seven brothers and sisters, and my folks own a buffalo ranch. We always had a generator for electricity because the winters are pretty harsh and the ranch is miles from anywhere. My whole family's used to hard work, so coming to Africa hasn't been that big an adjustment for me. Except that it's a whole lot warmer here," she added with a laugh. "Paul was raised the same way. We met in high school, and I never really cared about any other guy."

"Sounds romantic."

"I love him and we both love doing the Lord's work. Neither of us care that our kids are missing TV and car pools."

"I watch them playing with their friends. They seem very happy."

"They *are* happy. We'll go home because we want them to be educated in the States, but once they're grown, Paul and I will return to Africa. We love it here."

"I love it here too. And I always thought I could 'rough it' and not mind. My sister,

Amber, well, she'd have a hard time over here. No malls."

Jodene laughed. "There are certainly things I miss. Like snow. And cooking on a real stove."

"I—I guess I'm wondering if I really could give up the things I'm used to in order to live over here. Maybe I like my life of comfort more than I suspected."

"You're smart to examine your values before making a commitment to serve over here." Jodene toyed with her wedding ring, a simple gold band that caught the sun. "I'm guessing all this introspection has something to do with your feelings for Ian."

There was no use in denying it, Heather thought. "I *am* attracted to him," she confessed.

"As he is to you."

"You can tell?"

"Only every time he looks at you."

Jodene's comment made Heather feel good, as if an all-over glow had settled on her. "Well, we'll be going our separate ways in a couple of weeks, so that'll be the test."

"People do it all the time. They get separated by going away to college, or by being in the military, or by jobs in separate cities. If you and Ian want to keep the flame alive, you can do it."

Jodene paused. "What you have to ask yourself, Heather, is whether you *want* to do it. You're correct when you say this life is hard; it isn't for everyone, but the rewards are worth the sacrifice. And I'm telling you, a man like Ian will need one hundred percent dedication from the woman he chooses to work by his side. Anything less will rob you both. And make you both miserable."

Heather believed Jodene, and she wanted to talk more about it, but the teams trotted back onto the field, signaling the end of halftime, and Heather's questions were drowned in a sea of cheers.

After the game and back at the house, they all squeezed around the table—Paul's family and Heather and her friends. Plump roasted pigeons commanded the center of the table. "In place of turkey," Paul explained. "They're good."

Jodene also served large bowls of mashed sweet potatoes and green beans, platters of tomatoes, cucumbers, and lettuce, all fresh from her garden. "I saved the best for last," she said, setting down a bowl of cranberry sauce. "All the way from North Dakota, compliments of my mother."

Everyone stared at it for a long reverent minute.

"Here's my contribution," Heather said. The plate she set on the table held the contents of a full jar of peanut butter, beautifully sculpted to resemble a turkey.

"Wow," Boyce said. "Can I have a leg?"

He stretched out his hand, but Heather swatted it away. "Not so fast, buster. Where's your contribution?"

He grinned, reached into a knapsack, and pulled out an unopened bag of Oreos.

Debbie draped her hand across her forehead dramatically and pretended to swoon. "Be still, my heart."

The three Warring boys squealed in delight.

"They've had Oreos once before," Jodene said. "They've never forgotten."

With a flourish, Bob Hoover set a large box of Fruit Loops cereal on the table. "Barbara gave it to me when I left the ship. Part of our private stock."

The whole table applauded his generosity.

One by one, the others laid their food gifts on the table. A bag of microwave popcorn made everyone burst out laughing. "What were you thinking?" Debbie asked.

Jason Walsh, who was on the construction team, was the donor. "Hey, my mom packed it in my gear," he said. "Who knew I'd be coming to a place that didn't have stoves, much less microwaves?"

Once the table was fully laden and the laughter had died down, Paul said, "Let's thank the Lord for this wonderful bounty."

They all clasped hands and bowed their heads, and as Paul asked the blessing, Heather's heart swelled. She'd never known a better Thanksgiving. All the ski lodges in the West, all the fancy restaurants and banquets, had never been as wonderful as the simple pleasures of this table. For this table held not just food, but gifts gathered and offered from the heart of a family born not of flesh and blood but of service and commitment.

Once the table was cleared and board games were set up, Heather made up a plate for Kia, who was tucked securely under her cot. Heather tried to lure the child with Oreos and candy corn. Kia refused to take anything from Heather's hand, but once Heather set the treats down and scooted away, Kia quickly dragged them into her hiding place.

"There's too much going on," Jodene said, in

an effort to make Heather feel better. "She's probably confused by all the noise."

"Probably," Heather said, but she was disappointed.

Outside, night had fallen. Still in a mood of celebration, Paul turned on the gas generator so that they could see to play by electric light. The guests cheered, then took up a collection among themselves for Paul to buy more gas.

Heather thought of her family, wondered if they had gone skiing this year or opted to stay in Miami. She wondered if Amber was still on the outs with their dad, wondered if any of her friends had come home for the holiday from college. She wished she could call home, but of course, she couldn't.

"Checkmate," Boyce called out from a corner where he was playing chess with Bob.

Heather halfheartedly joined three others in a game of Monopoly. Dr. Henry and Ian should be returning at any time, and she was a bundle of nerves. She couldn't wait to throw her arms around Ian and tell him how much she'd missed him. Neither could she wait to see the baby and to show her to Kia. Perhaps seeing her rescued baby sister would be the breakthrough they needed with the child.

"You landed on my property," Debbie said,

intruding on Heather's thoughts. "Let's see, you owe me two thousand dollars."

Heather was paying off her debt when she heard a knock on the door.

"Enter!" Paul shouted.

The door swung open and Dr. Henry came inside. Alone.

The second she saw him, Heather's heart began to thud with dread. Dr. Henry's face was the color of chalk. Everyone in the room froze. Something was terribly wrong.

"What's happened?" Paul crossed the room with giant steps.

Dr. Henry looked at the group mutely, his gaze darting from face to face, his eyes tearing up. "There was an accident," he said finally. "Ian's plane has gone down. There are no survivors."

17

Grief.

Heather discovered that it had a taste: bitter. It had a feeling: cold. It had a color: gray. Grief was an abyss devoid of dimensions, and she was its prisoner, trapped within its life-crushing walls with no way out. Days later, she could not recall the sequence of events from Thanksgiving night. She remembered only images, snatches of questions and answers, sounds of crying. She remembered only pain.

Dr. Henry's story lay broken and fragmented in her mind. A Mission Air pilot, too sick to fly his regular route. Cancellation of the Tuesday flight. Ian, desperate to make it into Sudan and rescue the baby. A deal struck with a pilot of a two-seater plane.

Dr. Henry saying, "Perhaps it's best to wait until the DC-3 can go."

Ian answering, "Ed's expecting me. I need to get the baby out."

"I hear there's fighting. It may not be safe."

"It won't get any safer."

Ian's plane lifting off with an engine that sputtered. Dr. Henry watching until it disappeared into a cloud bank. Hours later, a mayday call from the pilot. Radio static. Radio silence.

Reconnaissance flights. A burned-out hole in a grassy field. Smoking rubble. No survivors. They'd never even made it out of Uganda.

For Heather, it was the end of a world of color and light. It was the beginning of her immersion in grief. Cold, bitter, gray, bottomless grief.

"Stay the night here," Jodene had urged. "You don't have to be alone."

"I'm not alone. I have my friends." Heather's teeth chattered, she was so cold.

Ingrid, Debbie, and Cynthia surrounded her all that night, and all the next day, too. They wept with her. And Boyce, Miguel, and Patrick came and took turns holding her, rocking her, weeping with her.

"He was my friend," Boyce said, his eyes red-rimmed. "I can't believe I'll never see him again."

"Not in this life," Patrick said. "In the next life."

Heather wanted to scream. She wanted Ian in *this* life. She wanted him now. She wanted to touch him, feel his skin on hers, hear him call her lass. It wasn't fair. *It wasn't fair.*

She knew that time passed because her friends told her when it was time to eat, covered her with a blanket, and told her when it was time to sleep. She did not go to the hospital to work. She could not be around death one more minute.

Dr. Gallagher came and talked to her, offered her some pills that made her sleep. He could give her nothing for the pain inside her soul. " 'The Lord gave, and the Lord has taken away,' " he quoted from the Book of Job. " 'May the name of the Lord be praised.' "

Heather tuned him out. God was cruel. He had no mercy. He had no pity. He had allowed Ian to vanish on a grassy African plain in a ball of fire. God could have prevented it but had not. Why?

One afternoon, she became aware that her roommates were packing. "We must go home on Thursday," Ingrid told Heather tenderly, as one might address a child. "We are packing up your things for you. We'll take care of everything. Do not concern yourself."

Inertia ruled her. Leaving seemed impossible, requiring more energy than she possessed. How could she possibly make it across two continents and an ocean? Listlessly she walked to Jodene's. But once she arrived, she couldn't force herself to step inside the house where grief had first assaulted her. The house would be filled with the sounds of the Warring children. Their laughter. Sweet, adorable, innocent children. With hardly a clue of the cruel sorrows life held.

She eased her back down the trunk of a tree, raised her knees, folded her arms, buried her face in her arms. Sobs racked her, heaving, gagging sobs that left her weak, as if she were being turned inside out.

She heard a noise, a rustling. Choking back her tears, she looked up. Beside her, in the dry dirt, Kia sat, staring at her through large brown eyes. Too startled to move, Heather let out a long, shuddering breath, half gasp, half moan. She braced her back on the tree trunk and stretched out her cramped legs. Kia did not scamper away. Instead, she lifted her hand and, with a feathery touch, ran her fingers down Heather's damp cheek.

"He's gone, Kia," Heather whispered in a cracked, thick voice. "My Ian's gone." She knew the girl couldn't understand her words, but it didn't matter. She had to say them, taste the finality of them.

Kia crept forward. Wordlessly she curled into a tight ball, lay down on the earth, rested her head in Heather's lap. Heather stroked the child's head, the smooth, soft skin of her face, the tightly curled hair. "You know, don't you, little Kia? You know how bad it hurts."

The hot sun beat down from the blue sky, on ground tufted with patches of green, on two people from different universes. "We're connected now, aren't we, Kia?" Heather whispered. In a cruel and hateful twist of fate, with a bridge of tears, grief had bound them together. Here, in the heat of the day, they had been joined, not by overtures of friendship, not by bribes of candy, but by loss. The loss of Kia's mother, of home. The loss of Ian McCollum, of love.

Heather's sobs quieted as she continued to stroke the child's head. The air settled around them heavily, like a drugged sleep. And Kia's arms drifted around Heather's waist, holding on. Holding on.

* * *

"You can't be serious, Heather. I won't allow it." Dr. Henry's expression looked both alarmed and haggard.

Heather was standing in his room, where his gear lay stacked, ready for the pull out in the morning. "But I *am* serious," she said calmly. "I'm going to get Kia's sister."

"But there's no time left. We're leaving."

"The baby still needs rescuing. I'm not leaving until I finish the job Ian set out to do."

Dr. Henry raked his hand through his white hair. "No. No, you can't do this. It's noble of you, but—"

"I mean no disrespect, sir, but I'm eighteen. I'm an adult. I can do what I want."

"I'm responsible for you." He shook his head stubbornly. "Your family is expecting you to get off that plane in Miami. What am I supposed to say to them?"

"This won't take me but a few days. I can catch a plane in Entebbe next week, after I bring the baby back. Tell my parents I'll call them from London. My sister, too; Amber is my sister. They'll understand." She didn't know if that was true, and she didn't care. After days of despair, she'd discovered purpose. She wasn't going to let it evaporate. Ian had always told her to help one by one. This was now her mission.

"But you don't understand what it's like going into a camp." Dr. Henry's voice turned pleading. "The camps can be chaotic, perhaps even unsafe. I can't come with you. I'm responsible for the others."

"I'm not asking you to come with me. I'm going by myself." She'd never dream of taking him away from his duty to the rest of the team. Bob Hoover was already gone, on his way to reboard the Mercy Ship on the way to North Africa, to be with his family.

"Who will be there to protect you?"

"Dr. Wilson will be there. Paul talked to him on the radio last night. He said Kia's sister's still alive." Her heart was hammering now, her body running on pure adrenaline. She hadn't slept all night, not since she'd devised the plan.

"Someone else will go—"

"No." She interrupted him. "There's no one else. I'm going. Paul will drive me into Kampala on Tuesday. I'll catch the Mission Air flight. I'll go to the camp, pick up the baby, catch a flight back. Two days is all it will take."

"Heather, please, be reasonable. It isn't safe."

She shook her head, spilling her hair from its

clip. Tension filled the room. "I can do this, Dr. Henry. I *must* do it. For Kia. For Ian, too. Try and understand. . . . I'm not afraid."

"You should be afraid," he countered. "These are dangerous times."

Suddenly, the image of a long-dead Persian queen, the Jewish Queen Esther, who had spoken up for her people, rose like a specter in Heather's memory, and she recalled Ian's voice.

At the door, she turned and said, "Well, Dr. Henry, if I perish, I perish."

Dawn was breaking when Heather, Jodene, and Paul helped the group load up two minivans for the drive to Entebbe airport.

"I wish you were coming with us," Cynthia said, chewing on her lip.

"I won't be far behind you." Heather gave her friend a hug.

For the most part, the group had understood and supported her decision to stay behind and go after Kia's sister. But now, saying goodbye, Heather realized how much she was going to miss everybody.

"It won't be the same without you with us," Boyce told her.

"Just don't pig out on peanut butter when you reach civilization."

"Never happen."

Ingrid kissed both of Heather's cheeks. "Take care of yourself."

"I will."

Boyce reached into his backpack and hauled out a gray sweatshirt with the words *University of Alabama* written in crimson block letters. "Wear this." He draped it over her shoulders and tied the sleeves together. "So they'll know what tribe you're from."

Heather smiled, squeezed his arm. "You'd better write to me when we're both home."

She stepped back and watched as her friends climbed into the vans. Dr. Henry was the last one to board. "I—I'll pray for you," he said.

She stood on tiptoe and hugged him. "I'm going to be fine. You'll see."

The vans slowly backed up, made a wide turn in the open yard, and started toward the road. The sound of the engines broke the stillness, while beams from the headlights bounced up and down, shooting streams of light into the darkness. Heather watched until the taillights were swallowed up in the distance. She felt Jodene slip her arm around her shoulders.

"Come on," Jodene said. "Let's go get breakfast. We've got a lot to accomplish if you're to leave for the camp on Tuesday."

Heather nodded. She felt momentarily lost, a stranger in a strange land. But the feeling passed quickly, and she hurried into the house just as the sun flared over the tops of the trees.

18

"Things are heating up in Sudan again, but stay with the Mission Air people and you should be fine." Paul Warring stuffed clothes into a duffel bag while he talked to Heather. He was driving her to the airfield in Kampala in the morning. He'd wait until she returned from Sudan with the baby.

"The Mission Air pilots are usually retired military," Jodene added. "Many have been missionaries themselves, so they're sympathetic to our work."

"In the old days," Paul continued, "it was the only way they could get around Africa. You've seen the roads, so you know what I'm talking about. A family could get stuck in the bush for months, so men took flying lessons in order to move around more freely."

"What about a ticket?" Heather asked.

"You'll buy it tomorrow at the airstrip. And you can pay for it with your credit card."

Heather remembered being surprised at the large number of banks and ATM machines in Kampala. But with the number of international travelers coming through Africa, it made sense. The universal use of credit cards made purchasing things a snap for tourists.

"How much money should I take with me?" she asked.

Paul and Jodene exchanged looks. Jodene went to the closet, took down a pouch from the top shelf, and unzipped it. She reached in, pulled out several coins, and plopped them into Heather's hand. "Take these."

"I have money. I don't want to take yours."

"You don't have these," Jodene said.

Heather turned the shiny coins over in her hand. "What are they?"

"South African Krugerrands—coins made of gold bullion. We keep them on hand in case of emergencies. In case something terrible happens to Uganda currency, well . . . people will always take gold in payment."

"I have American dollars—" Heather began.

"If you run into any trouble, all paper currency may be useless. *Goldspeke* is the universal language, trust me. Use it if you need it. You can pay us back when you get to the States."

Heather took the gold, knowing its value. "If I use any, you'll get them back with interest."

"We can't put a price on the baby's life, now, can we?" Jodene said. "Keep them close to your body at all times. When I travel, I put the coins in a pouch pinned to the inside of my bra."

"And don't let go of your passport, either," Paul said. "Keep it with you at all times."

As the seriousness of her undertaking began to sink in, Heather felt growing apprehension. This would be the only attempt to bring Kia's sister out of Sudan. If Heather failed, the baby would surely die. Heather knew that even if her mission was successful, there were no guarantees. The baby's cleft palate must be repaired, and Heather didn't know whether Dr. Gallagher's team could perform the delicate surgery in their less-than-state-of-the-art hospital. Everything would have to go perfectly if the baby and Kia were to be reunited and live happily ever after, Heather told herself.

As for Kia, she still preferred the underside of her cot to the run of the house, but she did slip out more frequently. Especially when Heather showed up at the house. Kia took candy from

Heather's hand whenever it was offered and had taken to following Jodene around the yard as she hung out laundry. Kia had still not spoken.

Jodene said, "You'll be taking boxes of medical supplies on the plane with you. That will be your entry ticket into the country. At the airport, you'll hand over the supplies to Ed and he'll hand you the baby. Then get back on the plane. These pilots don't stay on the ground long. They load up and return ASAP."

Paul took hold of Heather's shoulders. "In and out, Heather. That's the plan. Hold your head up and act confident. You'll do fine."

Heather offered a weak smile. "That's my line, remember?"

The three of them laughed. Jodene sobered and looked Heather in the eye. "Listen . . . we'll be holding a prayer vigil for you. From the time you leave until the minute you return, someone here will be praying for you. We'll pray that God's angels go with you and bring you and Kia's sister back to us safely."

Angels. Heather would never have thought to enlist the aid of angels. She couldn't help wondering where they might have been when Ian made his journey, but she didn't say anything. It hurt too much to even think about

Ian. She turned to Jodene and smiled with as much confidence as she could muster. "Thank you. I appreciate all the help I can get."

Early Tuesday morning, with the Ugandan children from the home surrounding them in the front yard, Heather climbed into Paul's Jeep, which was piled with boxes full of supplies. She wore an armband with a bright red cross emblazoned on it, a plain black baseball cap, sunglasses on a cord around her neck, and a small knapsack that fastened around her waist. "Travel light," Paul had said.

Jodene leaned into the Jeep, kissed her husband, and squeezed Heather's hand. "Go with God."

Paul backed the Jeep and pulled onto the rutted road. Heather hunkered down, folded her arms, and pulled the cap low over her eyes. The noise of the wind made it impossible to talk, so they rode silently into Kampala. Every mile of the way, Heather looked for some sign that angels were following them, but she saw nothing except charcoal fires beside the road as people stirred to start another day of hunting up food to fill their empty stomachs.

The Mission Air airfield was simply a grassy expanse with a couple of low buildings and a single runway. By noon, the plane was ready to go. Paul hugged her. "I'll be here when you return."

"Well, at least you won't be hard to spot," she said, looking around the nearly empty room that served as the passenger terminal.

Heather walked out onto the field and up the steps into the belly of the propeller plane, which looked like something she'd seen in an old war movie. Seating consisted of two long metal benches bolted along the interior walls. Seat belts clamped on from the wall behind the benches, fastening over her shoulders and around her waist.

Her fellow passengers were men—two World Health Organization representatives from Great Britain and several Africans. The pilot came aboard and welcomed them, saying the flight time was approximately an hour and that they expected no turbulence. He and a copilot entered the cabin, and Heather glimpsed a maze of gauges and switches. With the cargo in the hold and the passengers loaded, the plane's engines roared to life. Heather twisted to see the spinning propellers through the porthole-sized window.

The plane began its slow roll down the landing strip, gathered speed, and lifted sharply, clearing the tops of the trees surrounding the field. Heather's heart pounded as she waited for the plane to level off. Commercial airplanes made it appear so effortless, but this plane seemed to groan and clank like a tired knight in rusty armor.

The engine noise filled the cabin with a dull roar. The air was warm and close. She was glad the flight wouldn't take too long. When finally the plane began to descend, she braced for the touchdown. She felt relief when the plane rolled to a stop and the door opened. She descended the stairs into blinding heat. She put on her sunglasses and walked into a small building, trying to act confident and self-assured.

Heather fell into a short line to clear customs, which consisted of two armed soldiers checking passports. They looked her over as they stamped her passport. The automatic weapons in their hands were black, with tubular steel stocks and barrels. Leather straps held the guns across their shoulders.

On the other side of customs, she went to where the cargo had been piled on the cement floor. Her boxes were clearly marked with bright red crosses, but when she approached, a soldier stepped in front of her. He held his rifle at his waist and gestured for her to stand aside. He said something to her, but she couldn't understand a word.

"Medicine," she said in English. "For doctors."

The soldier glared and his weapon came up. Heather thought she might pass out from sheer terror.

"Can I help here?" A man stepped between them. He said something to the soldier in Swahili, and the man lowered his gun and stepped away from Heather and the boxes. Heather stood frozen in place. Her rescuer was in his thirties. He held out his hand. "Ed Wilson," he said. "You must be Heather."

She nodded, not trusting her voice.

"Let's get you outside and into the Jeep. I'll send my driver, Barry, in to get the supplies." He spoke to the guard, took Heather's elbow, and walked her out of the building. A Jeep with a Sudanese driver waited at the roadside.

As she folded herself into the back of the vehicle, Ed said, "Sorry I wasn't here when the plane touched down. We left in plenty of time, but some farmer decided to herd his cows across the road and held us up for twenty minutes."

"It's all right." Heather found her voice. "I know all about those cows."

Barry was loading the boxes in the back. Ed said, "I'm really sorry about what happened to that Ian fellow. Did you know him?"

A sharp pain sliced through her heart. "Yes," she said. "I knew him well."

"Then I'm doubly sorry. Rescuing this baby— we've come to call her Alice—hasn't been easy."

Heather looked around the Jeep. "Speaking of the baby, where is she? Paul told me you'd have her with you and all I had to do was get back on board the plane with her."

"Well, it may not be that simple."

Heather's stomach did a flip-flop. "Why not?"

"The rebels have gotten aggressive again. They routed a village less than twenty-five kilometers east of here. The military is crawling all over the place, which means they've clamped down on travel."

"Are you saying I got in but maybe I can't get out?"

"Yes, *you* can leave. In fact, that plane's returning to Kampala in fifteen minutes. It might be best if you left with it."

"But what about the baby?"

"You can't take her with you."

Heather couldn't believe what she was hearing. She couldn't have come so far to fail! "I'm not leaving without her."

A soldier began walking toward them, waving them off with his rifle. Barry started the Jeep. Ed said, "Let's get out of here."

They drove off in a cloud of dust.

"Where are we going?" Heather asked.

"Into a town near here, to a hotel where most of us health workers and foreigners stay. If you're here more than a few weeks, it gets old living in tents at the camp, so the hotel becomes our permanent quarters. The baby's there with Sister Louise, the nun who's been taking care of her."

The Jeep bumped along a rutted road, swerving to miss a child playing in the middle. Heather swallowed hard against a rising tide of fear and watched as the airfield, and her means of escape, shrank in the distance behind her.

The town was a dusty collection of buildings—shops, a gas station, and the hotel. Men lounged lazily against walls and along the roadside. Chickens ran in circles, pecking at the hard-packed dirt.

The hotel rose only two stories and looked run-down. Chipped pink paint flaked off the walls. Intense sunlight gleamed off a roof made of tin. A courtyard held small tables and wooden chairs, where several people sat sipping coffee. Inside the lobby were a desk with a clerk sitting idly, a broken-down couch, and a TV. Ed nodded at the clerk, who waved. Ed told Heather, "My room's on the second floor."

They climbed a flight of stairs and went to a battered door. Ed knocked lightly, then opened it with a key. Across the small room, a nun sat by an open window, reading a book. She rose and smiled. "So glad you're here, Ed. Is this Heather?"

Heather greeted her and looked at the bed, where a baby slept on a folded blanket on a mattress that sagged in the center. The room felt stifling, and noise from the street drifted upward.

"Still sleeping?" Ed asked.

"Like an angel."

Heather tiptoed over and peered down. Alice lay on her back, her small fists tightly closed. Her dark face, marred by the birth defect, looked peaceful. Instantly tears welled in Heather's eyes. She thought of all the people who'd stepped in to try and save her. She thought of Kia. They were tiny, defenseless children, caught in a terrible drama of politics and death that was not of their making. All they had in the world was each other.

Just then Barry eased into the room. "He's downstairs," Barry told Ed.

"Heather, come with me. We're going to talk to a man about a plane."

Down in the courtyard, Barry, Ed, and Heather took seats at a table with a small, dark-skinned man whose gaze kept darting around the open spaces. Barry made introductions, calling the man Mr. Oundo, Odo for short. "Sometimes Odo flies cargo out of the area for us," Ed explained to Heather. "In spite of difficulties."

Odo sat stonily. Ed began to talk to him in Swahili, but Odo kept shaking his head.

A man brought them a tray with coffee cups and set it on the table. Heather's stomach churned.

More discussion, but still Odo remained adamant. "Too dangerous," he said in English, surprising Heather.

"Does he understand English?" she asked.

Odo's gaze darted to her face. "I speak English," he said with an odd accent. "The problem is, I do not wish to risk my plane at this time." He started to stand up.

Heather felt as if she was going to be sick. He couldn't just walk away and leave her and the baby stranded. He couldn't! "Wait! Just a minute. Please . . . I have something to say. Will you listen?"

19

Looking reluctant, Odo settled back into his chair. "I tell you, it is too dangerous to fly. We can be shot down . . . like birds by a hunter."

Silently Heather tuned her mind to the only ear she believed could hear her. She prayed, *"Dear God, help me."* Gathering her courage, she said to Odo, "I appreciate your caution, Mr. Odo, but I really need to return to Kampala. Will you consider this?" She reached inside her shirt and extracted a small cloth pouch. She opened it discreetly and poured five gold coins into her hand.

Odo's eyes widened, then narrowed.

"If you take me and the baby to Kampala today, I'll give you these." She placed three of the coins in a line on the table so that they could catch the sun. "And when you come back, Ed will give you these." She handed the other two to Ed. "Plus," she said, watching Odo lick his lips nervously, "once the baby and I are in Kampala safely, my friend at the airport will give you two more. That's seven gold Krugerrands, Mr. Odo. Just for a short one-hour flight. What do you say?"

Heather's heart was thundering so hard in her chest, she was afraid everyone at the table could hear it. The air hung like a curtain, moved only by sounds from the street—the bleat of a goat, the *ding* of a bicycle bell moving past. Sweat trickled between her shoulder blades.

Odo reached out, but Heather covered the row of coins with her palm. "I'll give them to you tonight," she said. "After the baby and I are aboard the plane."

Time seemed to crawl as the man considered Heather's offer. An eternity later, he said, "I will take you." He turned to Ed, "Be at the field—you know which one I mean—at the hour of four in the morning. We must leave before the sun rises. If you are not there, I will not wait for you."

Heather watched Odo walk away, and she slumped in her chair.

"Let's go upstairs," Ed said. "Too many ears around here."

In the room, Alice still slept while Sister Louise watched over her. Ed studied Heather appreciatively, then shook his head. "That was beautiful, Heather. I was getting nowhere with all my pleas for humanitarian causes. He wasn't about to budge, either. Then you pulled the golden rabbit out of the hat and changed everything." A grin split his face. "Where'd you get the coins, anyway?"

Heather grinned ruefully. "An angel gave them to me."

He laughed out loud. "When I first saw you, I thought, 'What is Paul thinking, sending her? She's just a kid!' But you're no kid, Heather. You handled yourself like a real professional."

She felt as if he'd just held out a golden scepter to her. "I couldn't let our only chance for getting Alice out of here walk away. I knew I had to persuade him somehow. And my father always says money talks. So I thought I'd let it say a few things in Alice's favor." Heather sat cautiously on the bed, being careful not to wake the baby.

"Well, we're not out of the woods yet," Ed told her. "You'd best stretch out and catch some sleep. We'll have to leave around three A.M. in order to get to where Odo stashes his plane."

"All right," Heather said. She lay down

obediently, positive that she could never fall asleep, but within minutes, her eyes shut and sleep claimed her.

Heather woke to the sound of the baby's crying. Night had fallen, and a kerosene lamp lit the room. "What's wrong?" she asked groggily.

"Alice is hungry," Sister Louise said. "Come, watch how I prepare her food . . . in case you must do it."

Heather scooted off the bed. "Where are Ed and Barry?" The room was empty except for the three of them.

"Downstairs getting dinner. You should eat too."

"I'm not hungry. What time is it, anyway?"

"After nine," Sister Louise said. "Now, bring my little Alice over here."

Heather lifted the baby and walked to the dresser, where a small pan of water boiled atop a can of Sterno. "I'm saving the bottled water for you to take with you," Sister Louise said.

Heather watched as the nun poured a fine powder into the pan and stirred it until it cooled. "You want to keep it soupy," the nun said. "Like thin cream of wheat."

Next the nun picked up a large-gauge syringe from which the needle had been removed. She dipped the opening of the syringe into the gruel-like fluid, drew it into the barrel, and held it up to the baby's lips. Alice's oddly shaped little mouth grabbed the end greedily and sucked as Sister Louise eased down the plunger. "Now you try it." She handed the feeding syringe to Heather.

It took Heather a few tries, but she got the hang of it, and soon Alice had been fed. Heather held the baby on her shoulder and patted her back until she burped.

"Excellent," Sister Louise said. "We'll feed her again right before you leave."

The nun packed the small bag of powder in Heather's knapsack, along with a bottle of water.

Ed returned, bringing Heather a plate of *matoke* and rice. "It's all the kitchen had," he said apologetically.

"It's all right," Heather told him.

She ate. And then they waited.

Heather dozed, but at last Ed shook her shoulder and said, "Time to get going."

She gathered up her belongings while Sister Louise fed Alice again. Once she was finished, the nun held Alice close and said, "You be good for Heather." With tears in her eyes, she placed the baby in Heather's arms.

Wrapped tightly in a blanket, Alice seemed small and light to Heather, and she smelled of the protein powder she'd been eating. "She'd never have made it without you," Heather told the nun.

Sister Louise sniffed and stepped away.

"One more thing," Ed said. He took a small vial and a syringe from his pocket. "I'm going to sedate her. We want her to sleep for the trip."

Heather watched as he drew a few cc's of fluid into the syringe. He unwound the swaddled baby and stuck the needle into the fleshy part of her thigh. Alice wailed, but minutes later, her eyelids drooped and she slept.

Ed pressed the medication into Heather's hand. "In case she wakes."

Heather nodded, praying she wouldn't have to give Alice another shot, that they'd be back in Kampala before the sedative wore off—but also grateful for the weeks she'd worked at the Ugandan hospital, which had given her the skills to do it if she must.

"That's it," Ed said, glancing around the room. "Barry's waiting in the Jeep."

Holding Alice close against her chest, and without a backward glance, Heather followed Ed down the stairs and out into the darkness.

* * *

Without a moon, the night seemed impenetrable. The road was little more than a rutted trail, and Barry drove without headlights as much as possible. Although she'd wedged herself in the back of the Jeep, Heather bounced painfully. Her shoulders ached and her lower back screamed for relief. Sedating the baby had been a good idea. Alice slept peacefully, unmindful of the jarring.

"You okay back there?" Ed called to her from the passenger's seat.

Heather gritted her teeth. "Sure . . . but I'll probably need a kidney transplant when this ride's over."

"Not much farther," Ed told her.

The trail went up, then down. The Jeep slowed, then sped up. Heather completely lost any sense of direction. Eventually, Barry pulled into a stand of scrub trees and turned off the engine. Quiet descended. Slowly Heather's hearing adjusted to the hum of insects, then a faraway *pop, pop, pop.*

"Gunfire," Ed whispered. He stood up in the Jeep, peering off into the darkness. "Let's hope Mr. Odo's greed is greater than his fear."

Barry flashed the Jeep's headlights in three

short bursts. Heather's heart caught in her throat. What if the man didn't come? What if the rebels found them before they could leave?

From across the field came an answering burst of light.

"We're on," Ed said. He helped Heather from the Jeep, and while Barry stayed with the vehicle, the two of them ran, hunched over, across the field under the cover of night.

Mr. Odo, dressed in fatigues, waited for them. "Hurry," he said. He pulled branches off a large heap. Underneath was the smallest plane Heather had ever seen. He opened a door, helped her in with the baby, dropped a harness-style seat belt over her shoulders, and snapped it.

Ed reached in the window and took Heather's hand. "We'll pray for you and the little one."

"What about you and Barry? Will you be all right?"

"Don't worry about us. We're going away from the gunfire. We'll be in the camp reporting for duty at our regular time in the morning."

"Thank you, Ed, and tell Barry thanks too."

Ed moved back until Heather lost sight of him. Now she and Alice were together, but alone, with only a mercenary to shuttle them to freedom. She rotated her shoulders to ease her tension.

Odo settled in the pilot's seat and flipped switches, and the engine sputtered to life. To Heather it sounded like a broken lawn mower. "It can get off the ground, right?" she asked.

"Flies like a bird, lady."

She almost told him that penguins were birds too but couldn't fly two feet. Instead, she snuggled the sleeping baby closer and prayed.

Odo pulled on the throttle and the plane moved forward, bumping across the grassy field. It gathered speed; then just when Heather thought they'd crash into a clump of trees, the plane magically lifted. The darkness seemed to swallow them. She caught glimpses of the ground falling away behind them. "Pretty low, aren't we?"

"Have to fly beneath the radar," Odo said. "If the military sees us, they will shoot us down." He glanced over at her. "Don't worry, lady . . . we'll make it."

In the distance, she saw a reddish aura rising into the sky from the land. "What's that?"

"Another battle. A village burning."

Heather's stomach tightened, and she steeled

herself against images of screaming, dying people.

"Sit back," Odo said. "I'll radio Kampala soon to let the tower know we're coming in."

She reached into her pocket and removed the pouch. "Your money, Mr. Odo. I make good on my promises."

His fingers closed around the fabric, he jiggled it and, hearing the coins clink together, said, "You've paid much for so small a child, lady. And an ugly child, too. I do not know what makes her so valuable."

"I don't expect that you would, Mr. Odo. It's just that when I look at her, I don't see her body. I see her soul. And *that's* more valuable than all the gold in the world."

20

"It's sure taking us a long time to get to Kampala." Heather broke the silence between her and Odo. "The flight I took into Sudan only took an hour." It seemed to her that they were getting no closer to their destination, and the drone of the plane's engine was giving her a headache. The cockpit of the plane was so small, there was no place to rest her cramped arms. A few inches forward and she'd hit the instrument panel.

"Because we must fly lower, it takes longer to get where we're going. And my plane does not fly so fast. Don't worry, lady, Odo will get you where you want to go."

Heather gritted her teeth and tried to calm her nerves. Ever since she'd climbed aboard Odo's small plane, she'd been unable to forget Ian's fateful flight. It wasn't so much the radar and gunfire that frightened her as the memory of Ian and what had happened to him in a small aircraft such as this. Even the night at sea when the storm had raged had not seemed as long as this one. But that night Ian had been with her. She longed to have him with her now.

"Look," Odo said, pointing out the windshield.

To the east, the black layer of night was peeling back. The horizon resembled a cosmic sundae—a layer of pink, then one of gray, then a layer of blue black, and stars twinkling overhead like sugar sprinkles. "It's beautiful," she said.

For the first time Odo laughed. "Not at the sky, lady. Look at the ground." In the distance she saw flickering clusters of electric lights. "That is Kampala. Once again, Odo has cheated death." He sounded euphoric, making her realize how genuinely hazardous their trip had been. "I'll call the tower and get cleared for landing. What do you think of my little plane now?"

Relief flooded through Heather. "I think it's a wonderful little plane. The best."

"And Odo, your pilot?"

She sent him a sidelong glance. "The next

time I make a run for my life, I'll know who to call."

Still laughing, Odo picked up a hand mike and, in Swahili, requested permission to land.

True to his word, Paul was waiting for her at the terminal. "When you didn't get off that Mission Air return flight, I almost got physically sick," he told her after she'd cleared customs. "Then the news reports came about renewed fighting." He looked worried and haggard. "I knew you were with Ed and that helped calm my fears some, but, Heather, I've never been so glad to see anyone in my life."

"Same here. I would have called, but . . ." She shrugged.

"Yeah . . . no phones," Paul finished for her.

Heather turned the baby so Paul could see her. "Meet Alice."

"Hey, little girl," he said, taking the sleeping baby while Heather stretched her aching arms. "And this is my pilot, Mr. Oundo," she added. Odo had walked up after clearing customs.

Odo shook Paul's hand. "Thanks for getting them here," Paul said.

"We hid from the radar. It was a lucky trip."

Heather reached into her shirt pocket and pulled out another small pouch. "I believe I owe you this." Odo looked surprised. "Well, I couldn't give you *all* the money at once, now, could I?" she said.

He laughed heartily, as if she'd played some joke on him. "You are an okay person, lady. Very clever. Like a fox."

Once he'd walked away, Paul said. "I want to hear all about your journey, but first, are you hungry?"

"Famished. But is there anyplace where we can eat real food? I don't think I can manage one more plate of *matoke*."

He took her to a restaurant inside the Hilton Hotel in the heart of Kampala. Polished marble floors gleamed in the morning sunlight. Plush sofas and deep, cushy chairs graced the lobby. "I had no idea a place like this existed," Heather said, awestruck as she gazed around the lush atrium.

"You don't think wealthy tourists are going to stay at the Namirembe Guest House, do you?" Paul asked with a laugh. "I brought Jodene here for our anniversary. As missionaries, we're used to spartan lives, but every once in a while, we have to splurge."

The hotel was as opulent as any Heather had ever seen in the States, and she felt almost decadent sitting in such comfort, but after months of living in the bush, she couldn't get over how good it felt. She thought of the people she knew back home who honestly believed it was their lawful right to have running water and electricity. She hoped that when she did return to the States, she never took the blessings of her life for granted again.

"Let's eat," she said, picking up the menu and skimming it hungrily. Just then, Alice, who was lying on the seat of the booth beside Heather, began to stir and whimper. Heather lowered the menu and sighed. "After I feed Alice, that is."

It was midafternoon when they pulled through the gate of the children's home and into Paul's front yard. Jodene, the boys, and several of the older girls poured out of the house, everyone talking and laughing and raising their hands in gratitude. "When the two of you didn't get back last night, we feared the worst," Jodene said, hugging Heather. "Thank God you're all right. What happened?"

"I'll tell you everything, but I must do something first."

"Of course. You must be exhausted. Why not take a warm bath, grab a nap? We can talk at dinner tonight."

"That's not what I want to do first," Heather said. "Where's Kia?"

The little girl was staring from the window at the commotion in the yard. Heather lifted Alice off the Jeep's seat. The baby had slept off the sedative completely, and her dark eyes looked bright with curiosity.

Heather carried Alice into the house, and Jodene followed. Paul waited in the yard with the others. "Kia," Heather called softly. "I've brought you a present. Would you like to come see what it is?"

Heather crouched down, holding the bundled baby outstretched. Alice made a squeaking sound. Kia inched forward. "Come on," Heather said. "I've brought this present from far, far away . . . just for you." While she was certain Kia couldn't understand her words, Heather believed she could appreciate the softly urging, gentle tone.

Kia crept closer, until she was standing just out of arm's reach. She craned her neck to see inside the blanket.

"Just a little closer." Heather's heart hammered.

Kia dropped to her knees, leaned over the baby. She looked down. She looked up. Her eyes were round as saucers, and her mouth formed a perfect *o*. Then a smile, as bright as a thousand-watt bulb, spread across her face. She stretched out a finger and gently poked Alice's cheek, ran her fingertip across the baby's misshaped mouth.

"*Dada*," Kia said.

Goose bumps rose on Heather's arms. Kia had spoken.

" 'Sister,' " Jodene translated. "*Dada* is Swahili for 'sister.' "

"Yes . . . *dada*," Heather repeated, placing Alice in Kia's little arms. "Kia's *dada*. She's come back to you."

"We're going to miss you." Jodene came into the room where Heather was packing up the last of her things for her trip home.

It was days later, and Paul would be driving Heather first thing in the morning into Entebbe, where she'd catch the plane for London. "I'm going to miss everybody." She glanced around the room that had been her home for almost three months. While she missed her roommates, she'd been glad to have it to herself since returning from Sudan.

"Anytime you want to come back, you're welcome, you know."

"It may be sooner than you think. I talked to Dr. Gallagher and he's hesitant to attempt the surgery Alice needs. Says she really needs it done by a plastic surgeon with pediatric instruments." Heather flashed Jodene a smile. "I happen to know two very good plastic surgeons."

"Do you think your parents would come all this way to operate on one small baby?"

"We'll see." Heather was already plotting her strategy.

Jodene sat on the bed. "You know, there is one thing I want to talk to you about." She paused. "That's Ian."

The mention of his name raised the old, familiar hurt in Heather's heart. "What about him?"

"You haven't truly had time to mourn for him, you know. Once you're home, take time to grieve."

Tears misted Heather's eyes. "I'll always grieve for him. I still can't believe he's gone."

Jodene reached into the pocket of her skirt. "I have something for you." She handed Heather a book. "I found it in Ian's things when I bundled them up for Dr. Henry to give to Ian's father."

"What is it?"

"The journal Ian started for this trip. I

believe it belongs with you because your name is on almost every page. I only skimmed it, but when I realized what it was, well . . . I knew you should have it. Let's call it an early Christmas gift."

Heather ran her palm over the cool, smooth leather. "Thank you," she whispered.

"Read it when you have the strength. No hurry . . . you have a lifetime. He loved you, Heather. But he loved God, too."

Jodene left her, and Heather sat staring down at the book in her lap. *An early Christmas present.* Heather had forgotten about Christmas. At home, her family would be Christmas shopping. Familiar carols would be filling the air, and trees and houses would be decorated. On Christmas Eve she would go to the midnight candlelight service. And just before the congregation sang "Silent Night," the minister would read her favorite passage from Isaiah: "For to us a child is born, to us a son is given. . . . And he will be called Wonderful Counselor, Mighty God, Everlasting Father, Prince of Peace."

The miracle of Christmas was the gift of a child. The miracle of her time in Uganda was giving two children back to each other. Heather would remember forever the look of pure joy on Kia's face when she first saw her sister.

Had it been any different two thousand years earlier when shepherds, sent by a chorus of angels, came to gaze upon that other child? She didn't think so.

Heather wiped a trail of tears from her cheek and opened the book in her lap. On the first page, Ian had written:

The Journal of
Ian Douglas McCollum

On page two, she read:

June
I met a girl today. She was looking out over the sea, tears clouding her blue eyes. She was the prettiest girl I've ever seen. And surely God has sent her, for her heart is kind and full of love. And together, we will sail to Africa. . . .

ANGEL OF HOPE

This companion volume to
Angel of Mercy
is now available in bookstores.

When Heather Barlow returns from Africa, the joy and satisfaction she has gained from her missionary trip fade quickly. She is still feeling the pain of unresolved grief over the death of her friend Ian, and reading his journal only underscores her sense of loss. Now that she is back home in the United States, Heather feels directionless—unable to begin college, unwilling to remain at home with nothing to do.

While Heather has changed, her family has not. She is discouraged to see that her sister, Amber, seems no more mature than when Heather left, her parents no less involved with a medical practice that caters to the wealthy.

Heather continues to be haunted by Ian and what she learned from him—that one by one people can make a difference. Her sense of purpose is renewed when she persuades her mother to travel with her back to Uganda to try to save the baby she rescued on the mission trip. But when Heather becomes ill and cannot make the journey, Amber agrees to take her place. Now Amber must emerge from her sister's shadow to grapple with the age-old question "Am I my brother's keeper?"